Mountain
Madness

Christy® Fiction Series

Christy® Fiction Series

Mountain Madness

Catherine Marshall
adapted by C. Archer

Tommy
NELSON™

Thomas Nelson, Inc.
Nashville • London • Vancouver

MOUNTAIN MADNESS
Book Nine in the *Christy*® Fiction Series

Copyright © 1997
by the Estate of Marshall-LeSourd L.L.C.

The *Christy*® Fiction Series is based on *Christy*®
by Catherine Marshall LeSourd © 1967
by Catherine Marshall LeSourd

Managing Editor: Laura Minchew
Project Editor: Beverly Phillips

Library of Congress Cataloging-in-Publication Data

Archer, C. 1956–
    Mountain madness / Catherine Marshall ; adapted by C. Archer.
        p.   cm. — (Christy fiction series ; 9)
    Summary: Christy, a missionary teacher in an isolated mountain
cove, confronts her fear when she attempts to discover the truth
behind the terrifying legend of a strange creature.
    ISBN 0–8499–3960–7 (pbk.)
    [1. Teachers—Fiction. 2. Mountain life—Fiction 3. Christian life—
Fiction.] I. Marshall, Catherine, 1914–1983. II. Title. III. Series :
Archer, C., 1956–   Christy fiction series ; 9.
    PZ7.A6744Mo   1997
    [Fic]—dc21

                                                            96–38918
                                                            CIP
                                                            AC

Printed in the United States of America

98 99 00 OPM 9 8 7 6 5 4 3 2

The Characters

CHRISTY RUDD HUDDLESTON, a nineteen-year-old school teacher.

CHRISTY'S STUDENTS:
   CREED ALLEN, age nine.
   LITTLE BURL ALLEN, age six.
   WRAIGHT HOLT, age seventeen.
   ZACHARIAS HOLT, age nine.
   VELLA HOLT, age five.
   RUBY MAE MORRISON, age thirteen.
   JOHN SPENCER, age fifteen.
   CLARA SPENCER, age twelve.
   ZADY SPENCER, age ten.
   LULU SPENCER, age six.
   LUNDY TAYLOR, age seventeen.
   LOUISE WASHINGTON, age fifteen.

ALICE HENDERSON, a Quaker missionary who helped start the mission at Cutter Gap.

FAIRLIGHT SPENCER, Christy's closest friend in the Cove.
JEB SPENCER, her husband.
   (Parents of Christy's students John, Clara, Zady, and Lulu.)

AUNT BIDDY, relative of the Holt children.

BEN PENTLAND, the mailman.

DAVID GRANTLAND, the young minister.
IDA GRANTLAND, David's sister and the
  mission housekeeper.

GRANNY O' TEALE, superstitious
  mountain woman.

DR. NEIL MACNEILL, the physician of the Cove.

BIRD'S-EYE TAYLOR, father of Christy's
  student Lundy.

BOB ALLEN, keeper of the mill by
  Blackberry Creek.
  *(Father of Christy's students Creed and
  Little Burl.)*

EDWARD HINTON, soldier at the Battle of
  Little Big Horn in 1876.

MARY DAVIS, Edward Hinton's sister.

❧ One ❧

Teacher! Look out! There's somethin' dangerous lurkin' up in that big ol' tree!"

Christy Huddleston paused on the tree-lined path. "Zach Holt, I'm not falling for that old trick of yours again. That's the third time you've tried to scare me since we started on this nature walk."

"B—but teacher, I'm a-tellin' you for your own good!" Zach, a painfully thin nine-year-old, pointed toward the canopy of sun-dappled trees. "He's a ferocious man-eatin' monster. I'm afeared!"

With a tolerant sigh, Christy followed Zach's gaze.

"G-G-R-R-R-R!" A blood-curdling roar filled the air.

Christy leapt back as the growling creature dropped to the path on all fours.

"Howdy, Miz Christy," it said.

Christy grinned. She pulled a leaf out of Creed Allen's tousled hair. "Creed, Zach was right about one thing. You really *are* a monster sometimes."

"Was you afeared, Teacher?" Zach asked hopefully.

"Not a whit," Christy replied. "It takes more than that to scare me, Zach."

"She'll be scared soon enough," Creed whispered loudly, "if'n we get any closer to Boggin Mountain."

"Not that silly story again!" Christy exclaimed. "That's an old superstition, Creed. Boggin Mountain is not inhabited by some strange, dangerous creature. He's just a figment of everyone's imagination."

Creed did not look convinced, which came as no surprise to Christy. The people in this isolated mountain cove of Tennessee were full of superstitions. When she'd first started teaching, many of the residents of Cutter Gap had actually been convinced that Christy was cursed.

"Lots o' folks has caught sight o' the Boggin monster, Teacher," Creed said. "He's big and mean, with eyes like a bear's, only a far sight nastier. He has hair down to his knees, and teeth as sharp as huntin' knives."

"And he's a-covered with warts," Zach added. "Big 'uns. And he has a big scar on his head, and only one ear."

2

"Let's concentrate on things that really do live in these beautiful woods," Christy suggested. "Flowers and trees and all of God's creatures." She waved them off. "Now, run up ahead and tell the older students not to get too far ahead on the path. This is supposed to be a nature hike, not a race."

With a fond smile, Christy watched the two boys dash off down the thin path carpeted with pine needles. On her very first day of teaching, Creed and Zach had played a trick on her. Creed had tied a string to Zach's ear, jerking it whenever Zach told a lie. She could still hear Creed: "All them Holts, when they tell a whopper, their ears twitch. . . ."

Had that only been a few months ago? Yes, just last January. How frightened she'd been that first day! Sixty-seven students—she was up to seventy now—in a one-room school that also served as the church on Sundays. She'd had almost no supplies. And worse yet, no teaching experience.

Most of the children had never even seen a book before. And they'd all been so cold and hungry! Coaxing them to concentrate on arithmetic or spelling had been next to impossible.

Still, with the help of God, Christy had persevered. Trembling in front of the class that first day, she never would have believed that she'd have the courage to take seventy students on a walk deep into the Great Smoky Mountains. But here she was, surrounded by children like the Pied Piper.

Up ahead, she could hear the older children marching along, singing "Onward, Christian Soldiers" in measured tones. Behind her, a group of the smallest children was singing a silly mountain tune:

Call up your dog, O call up your dog!
Let's a-go huntin' to ketch a groundhog.
Rang tang a-whaddle linky day!

Truth was, her students were teaching Christy far more about the woods than she was teaching them. This lush, green forest belonged to these children. It was in their blood. They delighted in sharing its secrets with their teacher, the "city-gal" from Asheville, North Carolina.

"Miz Christy!" called Clara Spencer, a bright twelve-year-old. She was kneeling by a fallen tree. "Here it is! This here's pyxie lichen." She pointed to an odd-looking moss covering the rotting balsam log. "And that over there's reindeer moss."

Christy bent down to examine the delicate moss. "There are so many different kinds! It's amazing, isn't it?"

Clara nodded. "It's like that Bible quote about the lilies Miz Alice likes so much."

Alice Henderson had helped to found the mission at Cutter Gap where Christy taught. Miss Alice had become a good friend and advisor to Christy, and the children adored her.

"'Consider the lilies of the field, how they grow; they toil not, neither do they spin,'" Christy said. "'And yet I say unto you, That even—'"

"Solomon in all his glory was not arrayed like one of these," Clara finished proudly.

"See that pretty little flower over there?" Christy said, pointing. "Isn't that trillium?"

"You get yourself an A-plus, Miz Christy!" Clara cried.

"Your mother's taught me a lot about flowers on our walks together." Over the last few months, Fairlight Spencer had become one of Christy's dearest friends.

"Ma knows purt-near everything about these woods," Clara said. "Why, she—" A frantic shout interrupted Clara.

"Miz Christy! Come quick!"

Christy groaned. Creed and Zach were jumping up and down as if the path were on fire.

"What is it now, boys?"

"We found ourselves some monster tracks up ahead!" Creed cried.

"Don't you think we've had enough of that for one day?"

"I swear, Miz Christy! This ain't no pullin' on your leg. This is plumb serious."

"Could it be a bear?" Christy asked.

Zach shook his head. "Ain't no bear like I've ever seen. As sure as the sun's in the sky, Miz Christy. These is the tracks of a real live monster!"

"Creed, this joke is getting very old—"

"He's not joking, Miz Christy." John Spencer, Clara's older brother, joined the boys. His face was grim. "You'd better come take a look."

ꙮ TWO ꙮ

Christy ran up the path to the spot where the children were gathered in a tight circle. She could tell from their discussion that these were no ordinary tracks:

"Ain't never seen nothin' like it!"

"It's the Boggin, for sure and certain!"

"We oughta hightail it outa here before he comes to eat us!"

Several of the younger children were crying. Christy took Little Burl Allen's tiny hand as he sniffled. "Teacher," he sobbed, "I'm frightful scared."

"Don't listen to them, Little Burl," Christy said as the children parted to let her through. "They're just making up—"

Suddenly she paused. There, pressed deep into the wet dirt and pine needles, was the biggest, strangest footprint Christy had ever seen.

"Told ya it ain't no bear," Creed whispered.

Christy knelt down to feel the imprint. It was as long as her arm and half as wide. The four toeprints were the size of apples. Extending from those were sharp, deep claw marks. More footprints traveled back into the woods.

"What on earth is this?" Christy whispered.

"It's fresh," John said darkly. "That much is for sure."

Christy met his gaze. John, age fifteen, was one of her best students. He was tall and slender, like all the Spencer children, and had curly blond hair. Christy could see real worry in his light brown eyes.

"What do you think it is, John?" Christy asked.

"Creed's right. That ain't no bear," John said, scratching his head. "That ain't like nothin' I ever saw before."

"Could it be human?"

"That's not any human I want to run into," John said with a slight smile. "A foot the size of Little Burl, more or less, with four toes, and claws as sharp as an axe? No sir. I don't want to meet this fellow on a dark night."

Vella Holt had eased up as close to Christy as she could get. "It's the Boggin, ain't it, Teacher?" she asked in a trembling voice.

Christy hugged the little girl. "The Boggin is just a story, Vella. Like the haunt tales you children like to tell each other about witches

8

and ghosts and other such nonsense. He's just superstitious silliness."

"Beggin' your pardon, Miz Christy," said Ruby Mae Morrison, "but why would they call that mountain over yonder Boggin Mountain, less'n he was real?"

Christy smiled. "Didn't we just pass a stream called Cuckoo Jig Creek? Does that mean I can expect to find birds dancing the night away by the bank?"

Ruby Mae tossed her wild red hair. "Could be. Cuckoos is strange birds. Besides, this ain't like Asheville. When we visited there 'cause Betsy needed her operation, I read all them road signs. They're all borin'. First Street, Second Street, and on and on." Ruby Mae jutted her chin. "Here, names got meanin'. Pinch Gut's a squeezin' place between two rocky spots. Stretch Yer Neck Ridge is a place where you gotta stand on tippy-toes to see the view. And Boggin Mountain is Boggin Mountain 'cause that's where the Boggin lives. Plain and simple."

Christy stood, brushing pine needles off her long brown skirt. "Tell me this. Has anyone ever seen this Boggin man?"

"Lots of people have," Creed replied. The other students murmured their agreement. "My grannie saw him once, sneakin' out by our woodpile. Had eyes as orange as a harvest moon."

"Nope. His eyes are fiery red," Zach reported.

"My Aunt Biddie says so. She knows for sure, 'cause her horse got terrible spooked one day by the Boggin."

"His eyes are yellow," Ruby Mae corrected. "And big as plates."

"So I take it you've seen him, Ruby Mae?" Christy asked with a doubtful smile.

"Well, not exactly. But I heard Ben Pentland talkin' one day, about how he took a shortcut past Boggin Mountain to deliver mail to some folks on the far side. He was a-comin' home—" Ruby Mae lowered her voice to a whisper, "and all of a sudden, he run smack dab into a nest the size of a cabin. Made outa sticks and mud and bloody bones. And what do you think he saw, pokin' his powerful ugly head outa that nest?"

The children gasped. Christy groaned. "Let me guess. A very, very large robin?"

Ruby Mae rolled her eyes heavenward. "Miz Christy, for a teacher, you sure don't listen up when I'm doin' the lecturin'! It was the Boggin, of course. He had teeth as big and sharp as a bear. And a huge scar on his head. And his eyes, I'm tellin' you, were *yellow.*"

"That's why no one goes near Boggin Mountain," Creed explained. "The Boggin can swallow you whole in one bite, faster than a snake can suck down an egg."

Christy took a deep breath. How many times had she battled the children's strange superstitions before? She had a feeling this particular story was going to be difficult to put to rest.

"Do all of you believe in this . . . this story?" she asked.

"Not me," Clara said loudly.

"At last," Christy cried, "a sensible voice! Clara's right, children. The Boggin only exists in your minds. He's not real."

"I'm not sayin' *that* exactly," Clara added. She paused, looking a little uncomfortable. "I'm just sayin' if there is a Boggin on the mountain, he's probably just like any critter in the woods. Like a wildcat or a 'possum or an owl. You know. Just wantin' to keep to himself—"

"Clara," John said in a warning voice.

"I'm just sayin' that's what I think, is all," Clara said, glaring at her brother.

Christy sighed. "Sometimes we're just afraid of what we can't understand," she said. "Maybe next time we'll take a trip up Boggin Mountain and see for ourselves that there's nothing to be afraid of."

"I wouldn't do that, Miz Christy," John said quickly.

"Don't tell me you believe in the Boggin, too, John—"

"It's just . . . well, that mountain's mighty sticky climbin', 'specially in a long dress. That's all I meant."

"Please, Teacher, please don't make me go up Boggin Mountain," Vella pleaded.

"That ain't a good idea, Miz Christy," Creed said, his eyes wide with terror.

"All right, then," Christy said gently. "It doesn't sound like an easy climb, anyway. I promise I won't make you go."

"I got a question for you, Miz Christy," Ruby Mae said. "You say there's no Boggin. But how do you explain these tracks?"

Christy pursed her lips. It was a good question. "I can't explain them, Ruby Mae. Perhaps two large animals crossed paths and we're seeing a combination of tracks. Perhaps the imprint was much smaller, but the wet dirt allowed it to expand. It's been awfully rainy lately. One way or another, I'm sure there's a logical explanation."

Christy could tell from her students' expressions that they already thought they knew the explanation.

She started back up the path. "I think we've had enough excitement for one day. We should really head back toward school. Remember, stay on the path and keep an eye on your friends. No dawdling, and no getting too far ahead."

After a few yards, Christy glanced over her shoulder to check for stragglers. To her surprise, she noticed Clara heading deeper into the woods.

"Clara?" Christy called. "Come on. We're heading back to school."

"I'm just followin' the tracks to see where they go," she called back.

"You can do that another time," Christy said, this time in her firmest teacher-voice. "Come on back now."

Clara headed deeper into the underbrush. "Just another minute!"

"John," Christy said, "would you go retrieve your sister?"

Suddenly, Clara let out a horrifying scream.

Frantically, Christy and the others plowed their way through the steep underbrush toward the frightened girl.

Clara pointed a trembling finger at a small clearing in the woods. Impaled on a sharp, tall stick was a shocking sight.

The skinned head of an animal—probably a bear—was stuck on the stick.

Beyond the awful sight, the tracks disappeared.

"Explain that," Ruby Mae said in a hoarse whisper.

Christy had no answer. But little Vella did.

"The Boggin done it," she sobbed softly. "It's the Boggin for sure, and he's sendin' us a warnin."

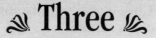

❧ Three ❧

I'm tellin' you, Miz Christy, that was the Boggin's doin'," Ruby Mae said that afternoon.

School was over, and Ruby Mae and Christy were the last to leave the schoolhouse, which also served as the church on Sunday. The teacher and student were walking the short distance to the mission house. Ruby Mae was the only student who lived at the mission. She'd had some problems getting along with her stepfather, and Miss Alice had suggested she stay in one of the spare bedrooms at the mission house.

"I'm not sure who did it, Ruby Mae," Christy said. "But I refuse to believe in some mythical creature who's been haunting a mountain for years and years."

They paused in front of the house, a large, wooden building set in a big yard. David

Grantland, the mission's young minister, was perched on a ladder, painting the frame around a second-floor window. His dark hair was splattered with white flecks of paint.

"It looks great, David," Christy called.

David wiped his brow with his shirt sleeve. "Yes, I'm quite the artist. I don't suppose you two would like to help?"

"But Preacher," Ruby Mae protested, "you're doin' such a fine job all by your lonesome. Me and Miz Christy, we'd just mess up your fine art work!"

David rolled his eyes. "Somehow I had the feeling that's what you'd say. Toss up that rag, would you, Christy?"

Christy retrieved the rag, careful not to walk under the ladder, and threw it to David. "Ruby Mae was just kidding, David. Is there something we can do to help?"

"Actually, I'm just about done. Although there is one thing—"

"Just name it."

"Promise me you'll never, ever send out letters requesting donations to the mission again!" David cried.

Some time ago, Christy had written several companies about the mission's desperate need for supplies. She'd asked for mattresses, paint, soap, window shades, cleaning supplies, food—anything she thought might make the lives of the mountain people a little easier.

To her surprise, she'd gotten plenty of responses. Week after week, Mr. Pentland had arrived at the mission with huge boxes brimming with supplies. Several months ago the Lyon and Healy Company had actually sent a grand piano. And the Bell Telephone Company had come through with wires and equipment for a telephone. That had been an especially exciting gift, since no one in the area owned a telephone. Most people had never even seen one before.

"So far," David said, "I've had to learn how to tune a piano and paint a house on account of those donations. Pretty soon, I'm going to have to figure out how to string telephone wires across a mountain. When I came here to Cutter Gap, I *thought* I was going to be a minister."

"The Lord works in mysterious ways," Christy said, grinning.

As soon as she was inside the house, Ruby Mae ran straight to the kitchen and began jabbering at high speed about the strange sights the children had discovered that afternoon.

Miss Ida, David's sister, was stirring a pot of soup. She was wearing a calico apron and her usual stern expression. Miss Ida was tall, almost gaunt, with sharp features and thin, graying hair. Sometimes it was hard to believe she was related to David, with his warm, brown eyes and friendly smile.

Miss Alice was also there sitting at the table, looking over the budget ledger, where she recorded every penny the mission spent. She was dressed in a simple blue skirt and a crisp white linen blouse. As always, she looked beautiful, with her clear, regal features and lovely gray eyes. Her hair was swept up in an elegant bun. Christy pulled a twig out of her own hair self-consciously. She probably looked a mess, after her adventure in the woods today.

"What *are* you babbling about, Ruby Mae?" Miss Ida said, clucking her tongue. "What's this about a bobbin?"

Ruby Mae sneaked a piece of carrot off the cutting board. "*Boggin*, Miss Ida," she corrected.

"Not that again," Miss Alice said, sighing. "I'd really hoped we were done with him."

"He left a footprint the size of a house," Ruby Mae exclaimed. "And a big ol' skinned animal head."

"You're exaggerating just a bit, Ruby Mae," Christy said. "Besides, I'm sure it was just a prank."

The screen door swung open and David stepped in. Paint splatters covered him like huge snowflakes. On the tip of his nose was a big white splotch.

"Looks like you painted more than the house, Preacher," Ruby Mae teased.

"David!" Miss Ida scolded. "I just washed this floor. Look at those boots! They're covered with paint!"

"Do any of you remember the story about the Little Red Hen?" David asked.

Ruby Mae frowned. "Is that in the Bible, Preacher?"

David bent down to unlace his boots. "No, Ruby Mae. It's the story of a hen who asks for help while she's baking bread. Nobody's willing to help her." He grunted as he yanked off one boot. "But everybody's willing to eat the bread after it's made."

"So you're sayin' you're the hen?" Ruby Mae asked.

"Exactly."

"But that don't make a lick o' sense. If you had feathers, Preacher, like as not you'd be a rooster, I'm a-guessin'."

David sighed. "Never mind. I can see my story is going to be wasted on you chickens." With one boot still on, he started toward the table.

"Preacher, stop where you are!" Ruby Mae screeched. She plowed into him, nearly knocking him down.

"What's wrong now, Ruby Mae?" David asked.

"Your boot!" Ruby Mae cried. "Don't you

18

know nothin' about nothin'? It's bad luck to step around with one shoe off and one shoe on! Every step is a day o' bad luck for you, sure as can be."

"That's nonsense, Ruby Mae." David gently moved her aside and proceeded to the table.

Ruby Mae watched in disgust. "I declare, you sure can be ornery, Preacher."

David took a chair across from Miss Alice and yanked off his other boot. "Where on earth do you get these notions, Ruby Mae?"

"Same place she learned to leave her old, tattered socks in the yard," Miss Ida said. "I was all set to throw them into that pile of rubbish you were burning the other day. But Ruby Mae would have none of that."

"Everyone knows if'n you burn a piece o' clothing, your body'll burn where the clothing was coverin' it. You didn't want me runnin' around with blisters on my feet, now, did you, Miss Ida?"

"Who tells you these things, Ruby Mae?" Christy asked. "I mean, things like the shoes and the socks and the Boggin stories?"

"They're just there, plain as the nose on your face." Ruby Mae glanced at David and giggled. "Or I guess I should say plain as the nose on *most* people's faces."

"Stories like these are passed from one generation to another," Miss Alice said. "I've heard the legend of the Boggin from dozens of different people. Many actually claim to have seen him."

"Where did they get that name, I wonder? It's not as if they've ever met him," Christy said. She rolled her eyes. "Listen to me! I'm starting to talk like this creature really exists!"

"But he does exist. You saw the signs yourself, Miz Christy," Ruby Mae protested.

"The name comes from the mountain people's Scottish background," Miss Alice said. "It refers to a ghost or goblin—a scary creature of some kind."

"And is he ever scary!" Ruby Mae let out a low growl, like a hungry wildcat. "That's how he sounds. Granny O'Teale done told me."

Christy laughed. "I can see I'm not going to get this superstition out of your head any time soon."

"You shouldn't act so high and mighty, Miz Christy," Ruby Mae said. "You've got your own superstitious side, after all."

"Me?" Christy cried.

David winked at Ruby Mae. "She has a point, Christy. Didn't I see you go out of your way to avoid walking under my ladder?"

"That . . . that's different," Christy said to David. "For one thing, I was just trying to avoid the possibility of your spilling paint all over me." She winked at Ruby Mae, turned back to David, and added, "I didn't want to end up looking like you!"

"And what is that supposed to mean?" David demanded.

"Go look in the mirror, Preacher," Ruby Mae said. "You look almost as scary as the Boggin."

❧ Four ❧

T he mountains are so peaceful at night,"
Christy said that evening.

Christy and David were sitting in old
wooden rockers on the front porch of the
mission house. Crickets chirped noisily,
while off in the distance, frogs carried on
busy conversations. The damp air was sweet
with pine. The Great Smoky Mountains towered around them, black silhouettes against
the deep blue twilight sky.

"I always feel so calm when I take in this
view," Christy said. "It's like a wonderful
painting that constantly changes."

"God's canvas," David said, nodding.

Christy turned her gaze in the direction of
Boggin Mountain. "I hate to think of the children fearing that mountain," she said. "It's
such a beautiful place, really."

"Someone had to put those tracks there,"

David said. "And the skinned animal head."

"Don't tell me you believe—"

"Of course not. I agree with you that it sounds like a prank. Still, you were right near the base of Boggin Mountain. And having these stories start up again is troublesome."

"What do you mean?" Christy asked.

"I'd hoped to get together some volunteers to help me string the telephone wires—now that I'm almost done with my painting project. We're having a meeting here at the mission house on Saturday."

"Will stringing the wire be difficult?"

"Difficult? That's an understatement. We'll have to cross Boggin Mountain, then go over Bent Creek." He shook his head. "If the men are worried about the Boggin, they may refuse to help me string that wire. And it's not exactly something I can do solo."

"I'm sorry," Christy apologized. "I guess when I asked for a telephone donation, I didn't really think about the complications."

David gave a rueful laugh. "How could you have foreseen that one of the complications would be a mythical creature with huge feet?"

"I'm sure this will pass," Christy said. "By tomorrow, the children will be telling some new ghost story."

"Maybe," David said doubtfully.

"If not, I'll try to distract them with a nice, exciting grammar lesson."

"You're a fine teacher, Christy Huddleston," David said with an affectionate smile. "But even you aren't *that* good."

～ ～ ～

As she got ready for bed, Christy mulled over her lesson plans for the next day. With so many students in one classroom, it was always a challenge to keep their interest.

She stared into her mirror as she unpinned her hair. She looked so different from the Christy who'd come here a few months ago. Her skin was bronzed, her hair streaked by the sun. She was stronger, too. Her arms and legs were hardened by the physical demands of work here at the mission.

Still, she loved Cutter Gap—even this tiny, simple room, so different from her lace-trimmed, lovely bedroom back in Asheville. Her room here was not luxurious, to say the least—a washstand with a white china pitcher and bowl, an old dresser topped by a cracked mirror, two straight chairs, the plainest white curtains, and two cotton rag rugs on the floor.

But the furnishings didn't matter. It was the view outside her window that made this room so special. Eleven mountain ranges, folding one into another, the summits reaching up as if to touch heaven.

Christy retrieved her diary and pen. She'd been keeping a journal about her adventures ever since coming here to Cutter Gap. By now her pen was almost worn flat. Soon she'd have to switch to a pencil—that is, if she could spare one. Even with the recent donations, supplies were hard to come by at the mission school.

She climbed into her bed and began to write.

I've got to find a way to get the children past this Boggin nonsense. I've seen the way rumors and superstitions can take hold among these people. It's no different, I suppose, from the rumors that old Mrs. Dottsweiler back in Asheville used to spread about the neighbors while she hung out her laundry to dry.

And as Ruby Mae pointed out, I'm not exactly perfect when it comes to superstitions. After all, everyone "knows" it's a bad idea to break a mirror—that means seven years' bad luck. Or how about going out of your way not to walk under a ladder? The truth is, I have my share of silly superstitions.

But this Boggin nonsense—that seems so much worse, if it gets in the way of something important, like the new telephone. I would hate for Cutter Gap to lose such an important connection to the outside world. Especially if it's because of some ignorant superstition.

When I think of little Vella's scared expression today, I just know I have to find a way to make the children forget about their fears. But they've learned those fears from their parents and grandparents, and I'm not sure if they'll be willing to "unlearn" them.

Suddenly Christy had a brilliant idea. If the children could learn from their parents, maybe the parents could learn from the children. If she got her students excited about the new telephone David wanted to install, maybe the children could get their parents excited.

And if their parents were excited, maybe they'd be willing to help out installing the wires—even if it did mean going near Boggin Mountain.

Now, if she could just find a way to sneak that grammar lesson in, too. . . .

❧ Five ❧

I have a surprise for you," Christy announced the next morning at school. "I know how disappointed you'll be to hear that instead of our usual grammar lesson, I have something special planned."

From under her desk, Christy pulled out two constructions of wooden boxes, paper, and string. She'd made them early that morning.

"What in tarnation are those, Teacher?" Creed asked.

"These," Christy said proudly, "are telephones. Well, they're not *really* telephones. They're practice telephones, until we can get the real thing. The Reverend Grantland is going to be putting up telephone poles and wires soon—hopefully, with the help of your fathers. When the new telephone is installed at the mission house, I want us all to be prepared."

"Teacher?" Little Burl waved his hand frantically.

"Yes, Little Burl?" Christy asked as she placed one of the makeshift "telephones" on her desk.

"Can I call my granny on that newfangled contraption right now?"

"That's not quite the idea, Little Burl," Christy said. She carried the other telephone to the back of the room and set it on a desk. "These are just pretend. You see, the telephone works by carrying your voice over a long piece of wire."

"How?" John Spencer asked.

"To tell you the truth, I don't know much about how they operate myself," Christy confessed. "I could try to find out more, if you'd like, John."

"Teacher?" Little Burl asked. "I figgered teachers knew just about everything in the world there is to know."

"Wrong, Little Burl," Creed said. "*Preachers* know just about everything."

"You're both wrong," said Clara Spencer. "In my house, it's my ma who knows everything. Just ask my pa."

Christy laughed. "Back to the subject, please. This box represents the telephone machine itself. The string is a wire. This paper cone is where you talk—the mouthpiece. And this other paper cone connected to the string is the earpiece where you listen."

"It's pure magic, it is!" Ruby Mae exclaimed.

"Now, the phones are really going to be connected by miles and miles of wires," Christy continued. "But I don't have enough string to spare for that, so you'll have to use your imaginations."

"Where do the wires go, Teacher?" Creed asked.

"Well, all over, Creed. But because Cutter Gap is in such a hard-to-reach place, with lots of high mountains, it's taken us longer to get connected."

Christy didn't add the other reason—that this area had simply been too poor to afford the luxury of telephones.

"My pa says those new-fangled contraptions is a heap o' nonsense."

Christy looked up in surprise. The low voice belonged to Lundy Taylor, a seventeen-year-old bully with a nose for trouble. Christy had suffered through her share of run-ins with his father, Bird's-Eye. Bird's-Eye made and sold illegal liquor—"moonshine." And whenever a fight broke out in Cutter Gap, you could always count on Bird's-Eye Taylor to be involved.

"Why do you think your father feels that way, Lundy?" Christy asked.

Lundy shrugged. He was a big boy, with dark, messy hair and a constant sneer. "Pa

says we got along just fine and dandy without no telephones for as long as his pa and
his great-grandpa was around. Says it's just a
way for you mission folks to sneak in with
your wires and poles and poke around
where you don't belong."

"But Lundy, that's not the reason for the
telephones at all. Suppose we desperately
needed supplies or medical help? The telephone is a wonderful invention, truly it is."

Lundy rolled his eyes. "Can't trick my pa
any sooner 'n you can catch a weasel asleep."

"Maybe so. But tell him to give this a
chance," Christy said. "Now, who would like
to be the first to try out the telephone?"

The classroom went wild. "Ruby Mae and
Clara. How about you two?"

Each girl took her place at one of the
"telephones" while the others watched, mes-
merized.

"Now, Ruby Mae, I want you to pick up
the receiver—that's the little cone-shaped
thing. Put it next to your ear."

Ruby Mae did as she was told. "Cain't hear
a thing, Miz Christy."

"Remember, these are just *imaginary* telephones, Ruby Mae."

"I know. I was just imaginin' I couldn't
hear a thing."

"Next, turn the crank on the right side of
the telephone."

"Ain't no crank."

"I know. You have to pretend."

Dutifully, Ruby Mae made a circular motion with her hand.

"Excellent," Christy said. "Now, in a moment, you'll hear the operator's voice through the receiver. That's me."

Christy went behind the blackboard and pinched her nose. "El Pano operator," she said in a nasal voice, sending the class into a fit of giggles. "To whom would you like to speak?"

Ruby Mae considered. "I'd be tickled pink to speak to President Taft."

"No, Ruby Mae!" Clara cried. "You got to talk to me, 'cause I'm the one with the phone!"

"I was *imaginin'*," Ruby Mae said. "After all, it's a purty sure thing President Taft's got himself a fine telephone. Probably one made o' gold. But if'n you're goin' to get all sore about it, I'll talk to you instead."

Ruby Mae peeked behind the chalkboard. "I don't rightly see as I need a telephone to speak to Clara, Miz Christy. Seein' as she's standin' right over yonder, clear as day."

"Imagine that Clara's in El Pano, miles away. You're here at the mission, and you want to tell her something very important. As the operator, it's my job to connect your phone to hers. I'll plug in the right wire to my switchboard, and, as if by magic . . ." Christy grinned. "R-I-N-G, R-I-N-G!!"

"Are you there?" Clara asked, holding the earpiece to her mouth.

"That's the receiver, Clara. And say 'hello' when you pick up the telephone. Try again."

"Hello? Is that you, Ruby Mae?" Clara said, this time speaking into the paper mouthpiece.

"It's me! Ruby Mae!" Ruby Mae cried, caught up in the fantasy. "And have I got news for you! The Boggin's a-hauntin' us. And . . . let's see. Last week in church, Granny O'Teale fell asleep and snored so loud the preacher said she coulda purt-near waked the dead. And Doctor MacNeill brought Miz Christy pink flowers the other day, for no reason. 'Ceptin' o' course he's sweet on her. . . ."

Christy laughed. "That's probably enough about my social life," she said. She should have known that Ruby Mae, Cutter Gap's biggest busybody, would instantly fall in love with the telephone.

Christy watched in satisfaction as the two girls prattled on. The grammar lesson could wait. For the rest of the day, the children took turns playing on the pretend telephones. Even Lundy gave it a try. Christy had rarely been as happy with one of her lessons. She might not have much in the way of supplies. But sometimes a little ingenuity was all it took to create excitement about learning.

❧ Six ❧

I know the telephone machine's a fine invention," Clara said that afternoon. "But I'm afeared it's causin' a heap o' trouble." She gave her brother a meaningful look. "If'n you know what I mean."

"Shh!" John put a finger to his lips. "The little 'uns will hear you."

The four Spencer children were heading home from school along the sun-dappled path that led to their cabin. Up ahead, six-year-old Lulu and ten-year-old Zady were picking wildflowers for their mother. Clara and John hung back a little so that they could talk in private.

"Trouble with you is, you think too much," John scolded.

Clara stopped walking. John could be such a know-it-all! She shook her head at her big brother. Like all the Spencer children, he had wide eyes fringed by long lashes. And like the others, he was dressed in worn but clean clothes, carefully mended again and again by their mother.

"All I'm sayin'," Clara said, "is it *could* be him doin' it, John. To scare people off." She chewed on a thumbnail, something she did whenever she was worried.

"Stop chewin' off your nails," John said. "Ma says you keep that up, one day you'll wake up without any fingers."

Clara rolled her eyes. John was only three years older than she was, but he liked to act like he was her pa. It drove her crazy.

Of course, the truth was, they were a lot alike. They were always thinking, always looking at things and asking, "How come?" They loved school, and they both thought Miz Christy was the finest thing to ever happen to Cutter Gap.

"You got to admit, it could be him," Clara said, sighing.

"I don't know," John said darkly. "Could be you're right. It's like you were sayin' yesterday, when we found those tracks. About how the Boggin just wanted to be left alone, like a wild critter." He gave her a playful punch in the arm. "'Course, you shoulda just kept your tongue from waggin'."

"It just plumb popped outa my mouth," Clara admitted.

"I understand," John said. He frowned, scratching his head.

"Stop scratchin' your head," Clara teased, "or someday you'll wake up and be bald as a turkey buzzard."

"Hurry up, you slowpokes!" Zady called.

"We're comin'!" John yelled.

Clara gazed upward. Through the dense layer of leaves, she could just make out the towering peak of Boggin Mountain. They passed it every day on the way to school. She used to think it was beautiful. Like a fancy blue-green party skirt, the kind she could only dream about owning.

Now, with all the latest scary signs, it was hard to walk past it without shivering, just a little.

"Clara, John! Come quick!" Zady cried.

Zady and Lulu were standing next to a tall tree, staring at something.

"It's proof, I'm a-tellin' you," Zady said when Clara and John reached the spot.

She pointed nervously. There on the tree were huge, long gashes. It was as if a giant bear had scratched his claws deep into the bark.

"The Boggin left it as another warnin' to us," Zady said.

Lulu clutched at Clara, hugging her close. "He's goin' to eat us all for supper!"

"Hush, Lulu. He ain't goin' to eat us, not for supper or breakfast, either," Clara said.

"How do you know?" Zady demanded.

"'Cause you're too bony for eatin'," Clara replied.

"It ain't like you've ever seen him. Besides, you heard Ruby Mae a-talkin'—"

"Ruby Mae ain't seen him, either. And you know she just likes to hear the sound of her own voice," Clara said. Ruby Mae was one of Clara's very best friends, but Clara knew her friend had a way of talking on and on without thinking things through.

"Look," John said.

Clara followed John's gaze. Hanging from a branch high overhead was a man's shirt—or what was left of a shirt. It was shredded into strips and stained with what looked like blood.

Clara shuddered. "It's just more tricks," she said, trying to sound calmer than she felt.

"I'm not never comin' this way again," Zady vowed in a trembling voice. "I don't care if I have to walk clear over to Wildcat Hollow and cross the creek. I don't care if it takes me four hours to get to school. I ain't never comin' past Boggin Mountain again."

Clara put her hands on her hips. "You can't take the long way around. Besides, even if this is the Boggin leavin' warnings, he ain't mad at us."

"Maybe he don't want us goin' near the mountain. He figgers it's his, and that's that," Zady replied.

"That's just plain stupid, Zady," Clara said, rolling her eyes.

"I'm a-tellin' Ma you called me stupid!" Zady cried.

"I wasn't callin' you stupid, I was callin' what you said stupid."

"Same thing."

"Is not."

"Is too."

John cleared his throat. "That's enough, you two. You sound like a couple o' hens cacklin'."

Lulu's eyes went wide. "Maybe . . ." she whispered, "maybe he don't want the telephones and all. Maybe he figgers this is his mountain to haunt, fair and square."

"That's silly, Lulu," Clara said. She met John's worried gaze. "Now, come on." She gave Lulu a gentle push. "Ma's goin' to be worryin' somethin' fierce if'n we don't get home soon."

As Zady and Lulu ran ahead, Clara turned to John. "How will we ever know for sure and certain what's behind all this?"

"If it's the Boggin," John whispered, "there's only one way to find out."

Clara gazed up at Boggin Mountain, looming above them. Today it certainly didn't look like the pretty party skirt she dreamed about. Today, it looked like a place where an evil creature lived, hovering in the darkness, waiting to pounce.

She tried to smile at John. "Come on," she said, swallowing past a lump in her throat. "I'll race you the rest of the way home."

❧ Seven ❧

I'd hoped to see a better turnout today," Christy said on Saturday morning.

"So had I," said Miss Alice.

"I'm sure the reverend did, too," said Doctor MacNeill with a shake of his head.

"Don't they know how important this telephone is?" Christy asked with a sigh. "I guess my telephone lesson with the children didn't have much effect on their parents. And this rain didn't help, either."

She peered out the living room window. Half a dozen men sat on the mission house porch, waiting for David to start the meeting. The day was gloomy. An early morning downpour had been replaced by gray drizzle.

Jeb Spencer, Fairlight's husband, poked his head in the doorway. "Howdy, Miz Christy, Miz Alice," he said, removing his damp, broad-brimmed hat. "Howdy, Doc. If it ain't no trouble, I was wonderin' if I might have a glass of water. As wet a day as it is, you'd think water'd be the last thing on my mind!"

"Come on in," Christy said.

"I'm glad you were able to come, Jeb," Miss Alice said as they headed to the kitchen.

"Wish more coulda come," Jeb said. "Puttin' up them poles and wires is goin' to be a heap o' trouble, I'm afeared. Hope the preacher knows what he's gettin' hisself into."

"It's my fault," Christy said as she poured Jeb a mug of water out of a white enamel pitcher. "I'm the one who asked for the telephone equipment. I guess I didn't realize how much trouble it would cause. Of course, this Boggin nonsense isn't helping."

Jeb took a long sip of water. "My kids saw another warnin' yesterday on the way home. Nothin' much—just some marks on a tree and a shredded-up ol' shirt. Still, little Lulu and Zady were mighty upset. Swore they'd take the long way to school from now on. Matter of fact—" Jeb shook a finger at Christy. "Weren't you headin' on out to my place today to see Fairlight? Maybe you should wait till I can walk you there, Miz Christy."

Christy gave a wave of her hand. "Don't tell me you believe in this nonsense, Jeb."

"I believe someone's tryin' to get our attention," Jeb said. "But that's all I know for sure."

41

"Jeb's right," said Doctor MacNeill. "These Boggin rumors come up from time to time, but nothing as persistent as this."

"Have you ever seen him, Neil?" Christy asked with a grin. "Or should I say *it?*"

"No." The doctor smiled back. "But I'm keeping my options open. I've certainly run into plenty of people in Cutter Gap who claim to have seen him . . . or it."

They walked out onto the porch. David was dressed in his old work clothes. He'd just placed on the porch floor a rough map he'd drawn. "I guess we can get started," he said, looking a little disappointed.

"There's some more a-comin'," said Jeb, pointing across the clearing past the church.

"That's Bird's-Eye Taylor and Lundy," Christy said.

"You sound surprised," said Jeb.

"I am. Lundy said his father isn't exactly enthusiastic about the telephone."

"And let's face it," the doctor added. "Bird's-Eye is not the first person you'd expect to volunteer."

"Unless you need help drinking down a jug o' moonshine!" Jeb joked.

"We'll take any able-bodied man we can get," David said. "We've got our work cut out for us." He pointed to the map. "We have to connect up to the nearest existing phone line. That's way over in Centerport."

"Three miles from the mission as the crow flies," said Bob Allen.

"Now, we can't fasten insulators and pins to live trees," David continued. "That means we have to cut tall, straight trees. Then we have to skin them and smooth them, lug them into place, and plant them up and down the mountains along the route. We'll have to hack off branches of any living trees that might swing against the wires, too." He stroked his chin, staring doubtfully at the map. "It's going to be slow-going, unless we recruit more men."

"We'd have more help," Bob said, "if it weren't for goin' over Boggin Mountain. Ain't there another way, Preacher?"

"Not without going miles out of our way." David shook his head. "Not to mention having to cross Dead Man's Creek. No," he sighed, "crossing Boggin Mountain is the only way."

"Only a fool lookin' for an early grave'll take that way," Bird's-Eye said as he approached. He had a shotgun slung over his shoulder. A big felt hat shaded his eyes from view. Lundy hung behind him, arms crossed over his chest, his wet hair plastered to his forehead.

"It's the only way, Bird's-Eye," Jeb said.

"Can I assume you're here to volunteer, Mr. Taylor?" David asked.

Bird's-Eye answered by spitting on the ground. "Not on your life, Preacher. You're a-lookin' for more trouble 'n you seen in all your born days, if'n you build that telephone contraption."

"Why are you here, then?" David asked tersely.

"Come to tell you what my boy done saw this morning." Bird's-Eye poked at Lundy with the muzzle of his shotgun. "Tell 'em, boy."

Lundy shrugged. "I was a-walkin' along, payin' no never mind, when all of a sudden—"

"Tell 'em where you was, fool," Bird's-Eye interrupted.

"I was over yonder." Lundy pointed toward Boggin Mountain. "With ol' Killer, my coon dog. All o' a sudden, Killer starts yelpin' and carryin' on like he's treed the biggest coon in all o' Tennessee. I look up, and hidin' on a rocky ridge is the Boggin. Big as all get-out, with eyes on fire. He aimed a rock as wide as that piano in the mission house right at me. Tossed it like it was the size of a pea. I jumped out o' the way, just in the nick o' time. Then I run home fast as I could and told my pa."

"And here we is to warn you, proper-like," Bird's-Eye added.

"Lundy," Christy said, "couldn't it have

44

been your imagination? Maybe the fiery eyes belonged to an animal. Maybe the rock just broke loose. It's been raining a lot lately. Mr. Pentland said he's come across some rock slides between here and El Pano."

"Nope," Lundy said defiantly. "I saw him, clear as day."

"Take my advice, Preacher," said Bird's-Eye. "You'd best be thinkin' twice before you head up that mountain."

"Thank you for the warning," David said. "But the mission is going to have a phone, if it takes my whole life to get it done."

"You keep this up," Bob Allen said ominously as Bird's-Eye and Lundy marched off, "you may not have a life."

"You're not scared, are you, Bob?" David asked.

"I ain't scared o' nothin', Preacher," Bob said. He reached for his hat and started down the stairs. "But I ain't no fool, neither."

They watched him leave. For a moment, nobody spoke.

"Well," David said with a grim smile, "I guess that makes the rest of us fools."

"What's that saying?" said Doctor MacNeill. "'Fools rush in where angels fear to tread'?"

"There's nothing to be afraid of," Christy said firmly, but she didn't sound quite as convincing as she'd hoped.

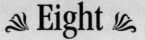

❧ Eight ❧

John? Clara? Is that you?"

Christy paused on the forest path. She was halfway to the Spencers' cabin and hadn't seen a single person on the long walk until now.

The two children hesitated, whispering to each other. After a moment, they ran to greet her.

"I'm on my way to your cabin," Christy said. "Your mother was going to give me another lesson about mountain herbs and wildflowers today. But the weather's so miserable, I guess we'll have to postpone it. Where are you off to?"

John and Clara exchanged a glance.

"To look for mushrooms," John said.

"To visit Louise Washington," Clara said at the same moment.

"Um, first we're gathering mushrooms,

then we're going to the Washingtons'," John corrected, "if there's time."

"I saw your father at the meeting about the telephone this morning. He said you and your little sisters came across some more odd signs on your way home yesterday."

"Up ahead aways, on the right." Clara nodded. "You can't miss 'em."

"Still, here you are. I'm pleased to see you weren't frightened off by this Boggin superstition . . . unlike most of the men in Cutter Gap." Christy shook her head. "Only a few people volunteered to help Reverend Grantland."

"Are *you* at all scared, Miz Christy?" Clara asked.

"Of course not."

"Not even a teensy bit?"

"Lots of things scare me, Clara. But the Boggin isn't on the list."

Clara chewed on her thumbnail, her thin, pale face tight with worry. "What *are* you afeared of, Miz Christy? If'n it's all right to ask."

"Well, that's a good question." Christy considered for a moment. "I suppose I'm afraid of not being as good a teacher as you all deserve, for one thing."

"But that's plumb crazy!" Clara exclaimed. "You're the best teacher in the whole, wide world!"

Christy patted Clara's shoulder. "Thank you, Clara. It makes me feel so good to hear you say that. Still and all, it's something I worry about. I suppose in a bigger way, it's a question we all face—are we strong enough to do God's work? That's something Miss Alice and I talked about when I first came to Cutter Gap. She said, 'If we're going to work on God's side, we have to decide to open our hearts to the griefs and pain all around us.'"

"So you're sayin' you're afeared of stuff *inside* you?" Clara asked, frowning.

"I suppose that is what I'm saying. Does that make any sense to you?"

"A little bit." Clara shrugged. "It's sorta like when we're learnin' arithmetic. I can see the numbers on the blackboard fine and dandy. But I can't always see what they add up to."

"Clara," Christy said with a laugh, "sometimes I feel that way about life in general."

John cleared his throat. "We'd best be gettin' on to the Washingtons', Clara," he said, a little tersely.

"You *mean* to the mushrooms," Clara corrected.

"Oh. Yep, that's what I meant, all right." John started down the path at a brisk pace. "See you later, Miz Christy," he called over his shoulder. "Tell Ma we'll be home soon."

Christy waved. *That's odd, she thought as she resumed walking. Clara and John are both acting a bit strangely. But then everyone is lately, it seems.*

She came to the deep gashes in the tree Jeb had told her about. Christy knew there was nothing to be afraid of. But she shivered just a little in spite of herself.

— — —

Since the weather was so damp, Christy and Fairlight spent the afternoon in the Spencers' tiny cabin, reading together from the Bible. When Christy had first come to Cutter Gap, she'd taught Fairlight how to read. Fairlight had caught on quickly, and now she read almost as well as Christy herself.

Fairlight was a beautiful woman, in a plain, simple way. She had a sweet, musical voice that reminded Christy of silver bells.

"Are you sure you can't stay a little longer?" Fairlight asked.

"I really should be going," Christy said, gently closing Fairlight's worn family Bible. "Miss Ida's baking pies all afternoon, and I promised I would help." She laughed. "Although my baking skills are so bad, she usually just shoos me away after a few minutes."

"It is getting late," Fairlight agreed. "Clara and John should be home by now."

"When I ran into them, they said they were going to gather mushrooms, then visit the

Washingtons. But now that I think of it, they didn't have anything to carry the mushrooms *in*."

Fairlight tapped her fingers on the worn table. She looked as if she were about to say something, then seemed to reconsider.

"Fairlight? Is anything wrong?"

"Nothin' much. I s'pose these Boggin stories have everybody a mite on edge, is all."

"Do you believe in the Boggin?"

"Nope. Them's just pranks, I figger." Fairlight gave a gentle smile. "And if there *is* a Boggin, I like to think he's just one o' God's wild critters, tryin' to get by, like everyone else." She shrugged. "Anyways, if you do run into Clara and John on the way back to the mission, tell them I need them to come home and chop me up some firewood and kindling. And I need it today, not tomorrow!"

Christy grinned. "Yes, Ma."

"I do sound a bit cantankerous sometimes, don't I?" Fairlight said with a laugh. "Just you wait till you have young 'uns of your own, Christy Huddleston! You'll see."

"But Fairlight, I already have seventy!" Christy joked.

Almost as soon as Christy set out for home, a light, cold rain began to fall. She hurried along the shadowed path, anxious to make it back to the mission before a real downpour began. The sun was hidden behind thick, gray clouds. Off in the distance, thunder rumbled, low and ominous.

On a day like today, the sweet peace of the forest seemed to vanish. It became a dark, frightening place, full of strange noises and leaf whispers. It was a place that made Christy long for the warm, cozy comfort of the mission house kitchen. She couldn't wait to get home, change out of her wet clothes, and warm herself in front of a crackling fire.

She passed the tree with the deep gashes cut into it. This time, she didn't let her gaze linger. Boggin Mountain loomed above her. Somewhere in the forest, a branch cracked. Trees rustled. Thunder grumbled, a little closer this time.

Christy forced a grim smile. It suddenly occurred to her that when Clara had asked what she was afraid of, maybe Christy had left something out. Perhaps she should have added hiking alone through a dark, rainy forest, full of unfamiliar, creepy noises.

Christy picked up her pace. The last thing she wanted was to get caught in a forest during a lightning storm.

Suddenly, her shoe caught on a tree root. Christy tripped, crying out in surprise. She landed on her knees in a puddle.

"Oh, no," she moaned. "My skirt!"

As she struggled to get up, she heard foot-steps nearing. They were coming from the direction of Boggin Mountain.

"Who's there?" Christy called. Her voice was just a thin whisper in the vast forest.

No answer. Nothing.

Still, Christy was certain she could feel the presence of another living thing close at hand.

Her breath caught in her throat. She could hear someone else—or something—breathing low and steadily.

It was watching her, whatever it was that was hidden in the dark, endless forest.

Christy didn't move. She seemed to have forgotten how to move. She peered into the shadows. A branch cracked to her right.

She looked, and then she saw it.

It was hideous. Monstrous. Its eyes glowed like an animal of the night.

It was the Boggin.

❧ Nine ❧

Somebody screamed.

A moment later, Christy realized it was her own voice echoing through the trees.

Then, as quickly as he'd appeared, the awful creature vanished into the dense forest.

Christy rubbed her eyes. Had she imagined him? Was she going crazy?

The creature she'd seen had been camouflaged by leaves and mist and trees. Christy *thought* she'd seen a man's face, buried in a mane of long, white hair. She *thought* she'd seen eyes, shining like tiny white moons. She *thought* she'd glimpsed a figure taller than any man she'd ever met.

She *thought* she'd seen it. But had she, really?

She tried in vain to brush the mud off her skirt. She peered into the woods one more time.

Nothing.

Just as she'd convinced herself she was a victim of her own imagination, Christy heard more footsteps.

But this time, she knew she wasn't imagining things.

"Clara! John!" Christy cried. "What a surprise! Am I glad to see you!"

"Miz Christy!" John called. He rushed to her side, with Clara close on his heels. "We thought we heard someone screamin'. Was that you?"

"I saw . . . I mean, I thought I saw . . ." Christy hesitated. After all her talk about the Boggin being a silly superstition, what could she say? *I saw the Boggin?*

"You look like you seen a ghost, Miz Christy," Clara said, taking her hand. "You sure you're all right?"

"I tripped and fell. Then something startled me," Christy said. She could feel her cheeks burning. "I suppose it was just an animal, watching me from the trees. But still, it did unnerve me for a moment."

"Was it the Boggin?" Clara whispered. She cast a nervous glance at John.

"I'm not sure what it was," Christy said.

"This thing, whatever it was . . . it didn't try to hurt you, did it?" John asked gravely.

"No. It just seemed to be watching me. When I screamed, it vanished." Christy tucked a damp strand of hair behind her ear. "Chances are it was just some poor, wild animal. I probably scared him a whole lot more than he scared me. I'm sure he didn't mean me any harm."

Clara stared off into the woods. "I hope so, Miz Christy," she said softly. "I truly do."

~~ ~~ ~~

The next day after church, Christy retrieved her diary and pen and went outside. The day was overcast, but at least the rain had stopped for a time. All of the congregation had headed for home by now, and the mission yard was empty and still. David was in his bunkhouse, Miss Alice was in her cabin, and Ruby Mae and Miss Ida were in the main house. Christy had the yard to herself.

She went to the chair swing under an old oak by the school. David had installed it a few weeks ago. He'd looped two long ropes over a thick branch, then attached the comfortable wooden swing.

Swinging gently back and forth, Christy opened her diary. It was so peaceful here, so calm. Her panic in the woods yesterday seemed silly now. And yet the experience had disturbed her more than she liked to admit.

Christy paused to gaze at Boggin Mountain, a silent, looming presence on the horizon.

Slowly, she began to write:

I haven't told anyone here at the mission about my experience yesterday in the woods.

I suppose I'm embarrassed to admit how afraid I was. Or maybe I'm embarrassed to admit how quickly I assumed that the Boggin—something I'd dismissed as a figment of Cutter Gap imaginations—was real.

Today, during his sermon, David talked a little about fear—about how, with God's love, we can overcome it. One verse in particular has stayed with me since this morning: "Perfect love casteth out fear."

I know that he was directing his words to the people of Cutter Gap. I know he was trying to convince them not to let their own fears and superstitions overpower them.

But as I listened, I felt as if he were talking right to me. I, too, fear the unknown. I fear what I can't understand. I fear that I won't be as strong as I want to be—as strong as God needs me to be to do His work.

And now, as ridiculous as it sounds, I have a new fear to add to my list.

As much as I hate to admit it, I'm even afraid of a creature lurking in the mountains I've come to love so much. The creature everyone insists on calling "the Boggin."

Ironic, isn't it?

Christy closed her diary. She smiled at the mountain she'd begun to fear.

She was going to have to go back, of course, just to prove to herself that the Boggin was nothing more than a superstition. It was an illusion—a trick of the eyesight and nothing more.

❧ Ten ❧

Boggin or no Boggin, it looks like you're making some progress," Christy said to David.

A few days had passed. David and his small group of volunteers had begun making telephone poles, cutting down trees, then stripping and smoothing them down. It was dirty, difficult, sweaty work. But slowly and steadily, they were making strides.

Most of the work was taking place in a clearing, not far from the base of Boggin Mountain. Christy had come to the site after school to deliver sandwiches Miss Ida had prepared for the men. At the last minute, Ruby Mae had decided to come along.

The truth was, Christy was glad for the company. It was the first time she'd been back to the area since her scare last Saturday. But just as she had promised herself, she *had* returned. Surrounded by the sweet scent of wildflowers and the merry discussions of warblers and tanagers, it was hard to believe she'd ever been so afraid.

"We've got a lot of the poles done, at least," David said. He paused to wipe his brow. "Today we've got seven men. Yesterday, we had three."

"Of course," Christy pointed out, "this is the first day it hasn't rained in a while."

"True. If the weather holds, I guess there's some hope we'll get this telephone of yours working before I'm old and gray."

"What's this I see?" Doctor MacNeill strode up, an axe slung over his shoulder. "Refreshments?"

"Miss Ida made sandwiches," Christy said.

"I helped a little," Ruby Mae chimed in.

Christy grinned. "Eating one of them doesn't really count, Ruby Mae."

"Doctor, any sign of . . ." Ruby Mae lowered her voice, "you know who?"

"No you-know-whats, no you-know-whos, no nothing." The doctor winked at Christy. "Sorry to disappoint you, Ruby Mae."

"Oh, I ain't the least bit disappointed!" Ruby Mae exclaimed. She shook her finger at him. "And I'm bettin' you wouldn't be actin' so sassy if'n you'd seen the Boggin for your own self, like some have." She gazed around the little clearing. "You ain't seen Clara Spencer,

59

have you? I coulda sworn I caught a glimpse o' her on our way over here."

"No Clara sightings, either," the doctor said.

"I'm goin' to take a look around. You keep a sharp eye out for you-know-who."

"Clara or the Boggin?" the doctor asked, but Ruby Mae was already halfway across the clearing.

"You shouldn't tease her so, Neil," Christy said. "She really is frightened. And who knows?" She paused. "Maybe there's more to this Boggin thing than we realize."

"Uh-oh. Sounds like Christy's been bitten by the Boggin bug," said the doctor. "It's turning into an epidemic."

Christy looked away. "I'm just saying we should respect people's fears."

"No," David said firmly. "We should help them fight their fears. After all, if Lundy Taylor can do it, anyone can."

"Lundy's here?" Christy exclaimed.

"Two of your students just got here." David pointed to two figures at the far edge of the clearing. Sure enough, Lundy Taylor and Wraight Holt were sawing away at a tall pine.

"Amazing," Christy said. "Especially after his run-in with the Boggin . . . or what he thought was the Boggin."

"He said he wanted to prove to himself that he wasn't afraid of anything," David explained.

Christy smiled sympathetically. It was the same reason, she realized, that she was here.

"Perhaps your lesson on telephone etiquette inspired him," Doctor MacNeill suggested.

"I doubt—" Christy stopped in mid sentence. Something was flying through the air at high speed toward the middle of the clearing.

"What on earth is that?" David cried.

"Well, it's not a bird, that much is for sure," said the doctor.

"It's a bag," Christy said. "A burlap sack!"

The sack landed with a soft plop. It was loosely tied at the top with an old rope, leaving a small opening.

"It came from over yonder," said Jeb. He pointed toward a stand of trees at the edge of the clearing.

"I'll bet the Boggin sent it," Wraight said. "I'd bet you my last dollar, if'n I had one."

"I hear somethin' powerful funny," Lundy said, taking several steps back. "Somethin' that sounds like—"

"Hornets!" somebody screeched.

First one, then two, then dozens of yellow and black hornets buzzed free of the burlap sack.

"Hornets!" Ruby Mae cried. "It's a nest o' hornets! And they is *mad!*"

In an instant, the air was alive with the angry insects, swooping in wild circles.

Everyone scattered in terror. The doctor

grabbed Christy's hand and pulled. "But the sandwiches—" Christy began.

"Come on, city-girl. When their nest is disturbed, hornets want revenge."

Christy and the doctor ran several hundred yards before coming to a stop. A few seconds later, a winded David and Ruby Mae caught up with them. A nasty red welt was already forming on David's right arm.

"Let me take a look at that," said Doctor MacNeill. "Anyone else get stung?"

"Not that I know of," David said, wincing.

"You know why this happened, don't you?" Ruby Mae said as she struggled to catch her breath.

"Because the Boggin's mad at us?" the doctor asked with a hint of sarcasm.

"Yep," Ruby Mae replied. "But the preacher went and made it worse by walkin' around in the kitchen with one boot on. I *told* you it'd bring you bad luck, Preacher."

"It's not me I'm worried about," David said gloomily, glancing back toward the clearing. "It's the telephone lines. No one's going to help me with this project now. Not after this."

―― ∼ ――

"Anyone coulda done it," Clara said.

She was perched on a fallen log in the woods, not far from the spot where David and the men had been working. John was pacing back and forth in front of her.

"Sure, anyone coulda done it," John agreed. "But who do you think really *did* toss that hornet's nest into the clearing?"

Clara crossed her arms over her chest. "How should I know?"

"You're thinkin' what I'm thinkin', aren't you?"

"Don't you go tellin' me what I'm thinkin', John Spencer. I got my own mind and you got yours, and that's that."

"You're thinkin'," John continued, "that *he* did it."

"I'm not thinkin' any such thing."

John kept pacing. "You're thinkin' he's mad about the phone lines comin' over his mountain, and people trespassin' and all. You're thinkin' he's so mad he just up and started doin' mean things to scare people off."

"You may be thinkin' that way, John. But I ain't!" Clara cried in exasperation.

John narrowed his eyes. "Then how come we came here today after school, sneakin' around like spies? We were lookin' for clues, Clara. Lookin' to see if he'd do anything suspicious. And sure enough, he did."

"I don't want to believe that," Clara said softly. Tears burned her eyes. "I *can't* believe it, John. It makes me afraid. And I don't want to be afraid of him."

"I know," John said. "Me neither. But facts is facts." He sighed. "Truth is, I think Ma's right, Clara. I don't think we should go back no more."

A tear slipped down Clara's cheek. "I reckon you two is right."

For a long time, John didn't speak. He sat down next to Clara on the log and draped his arm around her shoulder.

"Of course," he said at last, "we could ask Ma about goin' up the mountain once more. Just to be sure we're right about him. She could come, too. We got to know the truth."

"We could go tomorrow after school."

"Tomorrow it is."

Clara wiped her cheek and nodded. "All right, then. One last time," she said softly, "just so we know the truth."

❧ Eleven ❧

"Well, that's over and done with," David said the next afternoon.

Christy looked up from the papers she was grading. David was standing in the open doorway of the school. She'd just dismissed school for the day, and all the children were gone.

"What are you talking about, David?"

David strode in, leaving muddy footprints in his wake. It had started raining again that morning and hadn't stopped all day. The mission yard was full of deep, muddy puddles.

David sat on one of the desks in the front row, a scowl on his face. "The telephone. I'm sorry to report you can forget about having one." He combed fingers through his wet hair. "Nobody showed up to work today. Not even Jeb Spencer. Nobody."

"It could be the bad weather. Besides, after the incident with the hornets, I'm not surprised, are you?"

"I guess I'd hoped the men would find a way to see past it."

"It was all Lundy and Wraight could talk about today," Christy said. "Give it some time, David. Things will calm down in a few weeks."

"Maybe. But I doubt it."

"Who knows? Maybe it's for the best. I know the phone is important, but these incidents have been awfully frightening for these people." She gave a rueful smile. "Even for me, I have to admit."

"Don't tell me *you've* fallen for these Boggin stories, too?" David cried.

"Well, you have to admit there *have* been some strange goings-on."

David waved his hand dismissively. "Pranks. Probably one of our own students, just out to make mischief. Remember when you first started teaching? This same sort of thing happened."

"I don't know, David." Christy stared out the rain-spattered window. "The truth is, when I passed Boggin Mountain on my way to Fairlight's last week, I saw something . . . or some*one*. Whatever it was, it frightened me."

David leapt to his feet. He looked at Christy with a mixture of frustration and amazement. "I cannot believe you, an intelligent woman—a teacher, no less—are buying into this, Christy!"

"I know it sounds crazy, David. And it was probably just a wild animal. All I'm saying is that if I can be scared, as skeptical as I was about the Boggin, can you blame the men who were helping you? They grew up hearing horrible stories about him."

"I guess I'd hoped my sermon last Sunday and your talk with the children about the telephone would have some effect." David gave a resigned shrug. "Sometimes I overestimate the influence I have."

"It was a wonderful sermon, David," Christy assured him. "It gave me a lot to think about. It affected me."

David smiled wearily as he started for the door. "Not enough, I guess."

"David—" Christy began, but he was already gone.

She looked at the stack of spelling tests. She'd only graded half of them. Besides that, she still needed to work on her lesson plans for tomorrow.

Again she gazed out the window. She could just make out the dark expanse of Boggin Mountain. She'd always loved this view. On days when she'd feared she couldn't handle the challenge of teaching these needy mountain children, one glance at that mountain had always steadied her. It had been her source of courage.

And now she was afraid of it. She'd stay afraid of it, too, unless she confronted her fear.

In her heart, she knew the Boggin was a myth, a silly story, a figment of her imagination. But there was only one way to prove it to herself.

She wanted her calming view returned to her. She wanted her mountain back.

It would be hard, climbing on a day like today, but no matter.

She could do the lesson plans tonight. First, there was something else she needed to work on.

—◆— —◆— —◆—

"Slow down, John!" Clara complained. "I can't keep up. I keep slippin' and slidin'."

They'd climbed this route up Boggin Mountain many times, but today, the constant rain made every step hard.

John held out his hand. "Just a little farther."

"You're both too fast for me," said their mother, pausing to catch her breath. "Look at us, all a-covered with mud! What'll we tell your pa?"

"We'll tell him we got into a fearsome mud fight," John said with a grin. "And I won."

"I want to win," Clara said.

"We'll tell him it was a draw," said Fairlight. She sighed. "I hate keepin' a secret from folks this way. It just don't feel right. But I s'pose a promise is a promise."

"Ma?" Clara asked. "Are you afeared?"

"Don't worry. I'm here with you." She squeezed Clara's hand. "Come on. We're almost to the top."

They climbed on in silence. The rain made little tapping sounds as it hit the umbrella of trees over their heads. The ground was slippery as butter. Wet branches slapped at Clara's arms, stinging her. With the sun blocked by clouds, it was nearly as dark as twilight.

Clara wondered if they should have taken the other path up. It was much rockier, but it wasn't as steep. Because there weren't as many trees, John had been afraid someone would notice them heading up, so they'd come this way instead.

At last the trees began to thin. Rocks replaced the underbrush. Up ahead, nearly at the summit, was the place they'd climbed so far to reach.

It was a small, homely hut, even plainer than any of the cabins in Cutter Gap. On one side was a stack of logs. A small iron kettle hung outside the door.

It was a sad, run-down place. Seeing it

always made Clara glad for her own cabin, brightened by her parents' love.

But if the little hut made her sad, the space around it always made Clara smile. Hanging from tree after tree were the most amazing birdhouses Clara had ever seen. In fact, they were the *only* birdhouses she'd ever seen.

The first time she'd seen them, Clara hadn't quite believed her eyes. What a crazy notion, houses for birds! They had chimneys and windows and mailboxes and all manner of silly things a bird would never want.

Soon she saw that the wonderful carved birdhouses were like palaces to the birds who were lucky enough to nest in them. And she had to admit that the carving was something to behold. Finer than anything even her own pa could do—and he was the best whittler in Cutter Gap.

"Hello?" John called. He cupped his hands around his mouth and called again. No one answered.

"He ain't here," Clara said.

Cautiously, John poked his head into the little hut. When he looked at Clara, his expression sent shivers through her.

"He's gone, all right," John said in a whisper, "and so is his gun."

❧ Twelve ❧

Step, slide. Step, slide. Step, slide.

It seemed that for every step Christy took up Boggin Mountain, she slipped back just as far.

She paused, arm crooked around a thin pine, and tried to catch her breath.

John Spencer had been right. This *was* a tough climb. Especially on rain-slick rocks. Even on a sunny, dry day, this steep incline would have been hard. But today, in the rain, it was well-nigh impossible. She'd taken the longer, rockier route, hoping it would be easier. But nothing about this climb was easy.

Not for the first time, Christy considered giving up. She'd made it about two-thirds of the way to the top, after all.

And she'd proved her point. That was the important thing. She'd faced her fear.

Amazingly, she'd been more afraid back at

the school, just looking at this mountain. Now, as she struggled to climb it, all her energy was focused on taking the next step, and then the next. The notion that she'd run into some wild-eyed creature called the Boggin seemed almost silly . . . almost.

"Well," Christy said to herself, "I've come this far. I might as well go to the top."

She started her slow ascent again. She aimed toward a spot near a ledge of huge rocks. That would put her fairly close to the summit. When she got there, she promised herself, she could rest again.

Step, slide. Step, slide. This was crazy, all right. Brave, perhaps, but crazy.

The rain quickened. It was cold on her neck. The wind swayed the great trees around her. She was glad she'd borrowed Miss Ida's raincoat. Christy had told her she was "going for a little walk." What would Miss Ida say when she saw the mud streaks on her coat?

Step, slide. Step, slide. Suddenly Christy heard a strange grinding noise.

She looked up to see a great boulder tumbling down the mountain. It hit a tree, then another, then continued on its way.

There'd been rock slides recently because of all the rain, Christy recalled with a jolt. She stood rigidly, her heart pounding, her fists clenched.

Was that all? Just one boulder and nothing more? Was it safe to go on?

She took another tentative step, and then it happened.

With a thunderous crash, the rocky ledge crumbled like a tower of children's blocks. Tiny pebbles and giant, sharp rocks began to roll down the mountain. Boulders bounced as if they were rubber balls.

Christy spun around. She cut to her left, running down the mountain as fast as she could, hoping the slide would pass right by her.

Out of the corner of her eye, she saw a huge boulder hit a pine tree dead-on. The tree splintered with a horrible cracking sound, then began to fall.

She slipped, righted herself, and kept running. Her lungs burned. Just a little farther, she told herself, and she'd be safe.

The boulders rolled and crashed and thudded. Most were to her right, but some seemed to be directly behind her.

She wanted to turn to look. But there wasn't time. She had to run. She had to keep running.

Her skirt caught on a prickly shrub. She yanked it free. She stumbled. She ran another step.

And then she knew it was coming for her.

She heard the terrifying crash as the giant boulder hit a tree trunk directly behind her.

The tree snapped like a toothpick. Christy felt its shadow over her as it fell.

She looked up. She tripped. As the tree toppled, so did she.

She tried to crawl, but the tree was coming down too fast.

There was nothing else to do. Christy closed her eyes and covered her head. As she waited to die, she prayed.

❧ Thirteen ❧

Slowly, Christy opened her eyes.

She wasn't dead.

In fact, she was very much alive.

She tried to move but couldn't. Sweet-smelling needles tickled her nose. She was trapped in the great arms of a massive pine tree.

Christy lifted her head. She could just make out the huge boulder that had tumbled the tree. It was wedged against what was left of the trunk.

She wondered how badly she was hurt. She had some scrapes on her face and hands, and her right ankle throbbed, but she doubted any bones had been broken.

With all her might, Christy struggled to break free of the big tree's grasp. The massive trunk lay just inches to her left. Another foot and it would have landed directly on top of her.

It was a miracle that she hadn't been crushed.

"Thank you, God," Christy whispered.

Again she tried to free herself from the piney trap, but it was no use. The tree was huge, and she was not.

Suddenly, to her surprise, Christy found herself laughing. Now that she was out of danger, her predicament almost seemed ridiculous.

She could just see the surprise on the faces of her rescuers when they found her! Christy Huddleston, trapped by a man-eating pine tree. She'd gotten into plenty of hair-raising scrapes since coming to Cutter Gap. But Doctor MacNeill would tease her for weeks over this one.

Unless . . .

Christy gulped. Unless no one found her. Unless no one would even think to look for her here on Boggin Mountain.

After all, she hadn't told anyone where she was going. All she'd said to Miss Ida was that she was going for a walk. But nobody would expect Christy to have headed for the summit of Boggin Mountain. Nobody.

How long could she last out here without food, exposed to the elements? The awful possibilities marched through her head like an army. What if it stormed? How cold would it get at night? What if a hungry animal found her?

She could scream for help, but what would be the point?

No one came near this place. Everyone in Cutter Gap feared it.

She could scream till her voice gave out, and the only ones to hear it would be the wild creatures hidden in the trees.

And, of course, the Boggin.

"No!" Christy said out loud, trying to calm her frantic heart. "I am going to be fine! And there is no Boggin! The Boggin does not exist!"

Hearing the words made her feel better. She'd come here to conquer her fear, after all. She wasn't going to give in to it all over again. Especially not now, when she needed to keep her wits about her.

"Well, if no one's going to show up to rescue me," Christy said aloud, "I guess I'm going to have to rescue myself."

She felt a little silly, talking to herself. But the sound of a human voice—even it was just her own—was somehow reassuring.

Lifting her head a couple inches, Christy surveyed her situation. She was pinned down by layer upon layer of branches—some thick, some not-so-thick. Her only hope seemed to be to try to crawl her way out, inch by precious inch.

But that was easier said than done.

As she struggled to move, Christy began to sing an old song she'd loved as a child. It had helped her through many frightening moments. In fact, it was one of the first things she'd taught her students here in Cutter Gap:

> *God will take care of you*
> *Through every day, o'er all the way,*
> *He will take care of you,*
> *He will take care of you.*

She'd just started to sing it again when the loud snap of a twig silenced her. *She* hadn't broken it. Someone in the woods had.

"Is anybody there?" Christy called. "Please help me! I'm over here, trapped under this pine tree."

She paused. Nobody replied. Perhaps it had just been an animal passing by.

Still, Christy had the same eerie feeling she'd had that day on the path, when she'd been certain she'd spotted the Boggin. The sense that she was being watched. The feeling that there was another presence lurking nearby.

"Hello?" Christy called again.

She struggled to lift her head. She looked to the left. She looked to the right. And then she saw him.

He was only a few feet away from her. He towered over the fallen tree like some awful giant out of a fairy tale. He was clearly old.

His hair and beard were long and white, hanging in wisps down to his shoulders.

A horrible scar extended from his cheek to the spot where his right ear would have been. Even with his mane of hair, Christy could see that the ear was gone.

But it was his eyes that Christy focused on. They were the eyes of an old man, milky with disease, shining like white moons.

They were the eyes of the man she'd seen that day on the path.

"You're the Boggin," Christy whispered.

He came closer in two great strides. Only then did Christy see the gun and large hunting knife tucked into his belt.

Christy stared in horror at the hideous creature towering over her. "Please don't hurt me," she begged in a terrified whisper.

He didn't respond. For a moment, he didn't even move.

Suddenly, he lunged toward Christy. She let out a scream before realizing that he was reaching for a branch of the fallen tree.

To her amazement, Christy felt the weight of the tree easing. The old man could only lift the branches a few inches. But it was just enough to allow Christy the room she needed to crawl free.

When she was safe, the Boggin released the tree. Christy smiled at him. "Thank you so much," she said. "If you hadn't come along, I don't know what I would have done."

When he didn't answer, she wondered if he couldn't speak. He was staring at her with the same curiosity and fear he was probably seeing on her own face.

"You're the teacher," he finally said.

"Yes," she replied in surprise. "How did you know that?"

He didn't answer. "Can you walk?" he asked.

"I'm not sure. I think I may have hurt my ankle. Not to mention Miss Ida's coat."

Christy tried to stand, but her swollen ankle would not take any weight.

"I'll help you," said the Boggin.

"Really, I'm fine."

"You can come to my hut."

"No," Christy said, a little frantically. "I . . . I need to go home."

"I'll wrap up your ankle so you can walk on it," said the Boggin, as certainly as if he were Doctor MacNeill. "It's a long way down, Miz Huddleston."

Christy took a deep breath. This was the Boggin she was talking to. The creature of nightmares and superstitious stories. This was the Boggin, inviting her to his hut so he could tend to her ankle. And he knew her name.

"I . . . I don't even know your name, but you know mine," Christy said.

For the first time, the old man showed a hint of a smile.

"My real name don't matter no more," he said. "Boggin'll do just fine."

Fourteen

Christy and the Boggin made their way to the top of the mountain, step by slow step. She leaned on the tall old man for support, amazed at his strength. Twice Christy tried to start a conversation, but her questions were met with silence.

She had so many questions, too. Was he a hermit? How did he know her name? Was he the one who'd been frightening the people of Cutter Gap? And if so, why?

As they neared the summit, Christy thought she heard voices.

"Did you hear that?" she asked the Boggin.

He nodded. "My friends," was all he said.

The Boggin had friends? Christy thought in disbelief. As far as she knew, everyone in Cutter Gap feared him. How could he have any friends?

Up ahead, a tiny hut in a clearing came

into view. And then Christy saw who the Boggin's friends were.

"Edward! Christy!" Fairlight said. "Are you hurt?"

John and Clara ran to help Christy the rest of the way. "There was a rock slide," Christy explained. "A pine tree practically fell right on top of me. The Bog—" she stopped herself, "*Edward* saved me."

The old man shrugged. "I guess I might as well introduce myself formal-like, after all. My name's Edward Hinton."

"Edward Hinton," Christy repeated. "I like that much better than 'the Boggin.'"

"Me, too, I reckon."

"What on earth are you three doing here?" Christy asked.

Fairlight glanced at Edward. "That's a long story, I reckon. First things first. It sure looks to me like you need to set down and let me tend to that foot."

Clara retrieved a chair from the hut and Christy sat down gratefully. The hut, Christy noticed, was very small and crudely made. But surrounding it, dangling off of every tree limb, it seemed, were the most beautiful birdhouses Christy had ever seen.

Some looked like the elaborate Victorian homes back in Asheville. Some looked like the brick row houses in Boston Christy had seen pictures of in books. One even looked like the White House. And all of them seemed to be occupied by very happy birds.

"Those birdhouses," Christy said, shaking her head in wonder. "They're so beautiful!"

"Ain't they the purtiest things you ever did set eyes on, Miz Christy?" Clara exclaimed. "Edward made 'em all."

"They're amazing," Christy replied. "Just amazing."

"I whittle to while away the time," the old man said. "Tain't nothin' too special. I used to make 'em more fancy-like. But the eyes are goin' now. I have to go by feel more 'n sight when I'm whittlin' the little things."

Quiet fell for a moment, broken only by the happy chattering of the birds in their custom-made homes. Edward cleared his throat. "I guess I'll be gettin' you somethin' to wrap up that ankle with." He knocked his head with his hand. "Listen to me! I plumb forgot my manners, I ain't had company in so long—'ceptin' of course for Clara and John and their ma. Can I fetch you somethin' to drink? Or maybe to eat? I got some fresh fish I was goin' to fry up."

"No, thank you, Edward. But I do have some questions I'd like you to answer, if you'd be so kind."

Edward sighed. "Now I remember why I don't much like company," he said wryly, and with that, he disappeared into his tiny hut.

Christy looked at Fairlight and the children expectantly. "Well? Are you three going to explain to me why you just happen to be on the top of Boggin Mountain? What's this all about, anyway?"

Clara sighed. "Like Ma said, it's kind of a long story, Miz Christy."

"I have plenty of time."

"See, Edward's our friend," Clara said softly. "We met him one day pickin' flowers with Ma. Usually we never came up on Boggin Mountain, 'cause of all the stories and all."

"But that day, we kinda got carried away, lookin' for jack-in-the-pulpits," Fairlight said.

"Anyways, I found this baby wren on the ground, sickly as could be," Clara continued. "No ma, no nest in sight. And just as I knelt down to get her, I saw Edward. I like to nearly jumped outa my skin—" she lowered her voice, "'cause o' the way he looks and all. But he picked up that baby wren, gentle as could be, and took her back to his place, and fixed her up as good as new." She smiled. "And that's how we got to be friends with Edward."

"Why didn't you tell anyone?" Christy asked, leaning down to rub her tender ankle. "All those stories about the Boggin. They could have been put to rest for good."

"Ma and Clara and me promised we wouldn't tell anyone we'd met him. Edward just wants to be left alone, Miz Christy," John said quietly.

"But why?"

The old man appeared in the doorway of the hut. He was holding a strip of white cloth. "Because he doesn't much like people," he explained. His voice was bitter. "Because when you keep to yourself, no harm can come to you."

"But Clara and John and Fairlight are your friends," Christy pointed out.

"They're different," Edward said. "They're the exception that proves the rule."

Christy frowned. "Is that why you've been terrorizing everyone in Cutter Gap?" she demanded.

"I got nothin' to do with that," Edward said angrily. "The children told me about those goings-on last time they came to visit."

"But who else could be doing it, Edward?" Clara asked softly. "I mean, we've kinda plumb run out o' answers. That's why John and me and Ma come back today, to ask . . ."

"Ask what?" Edward crossed his arms over his chest.

"We were just thinkin' maybe with the telephone comin' and all . . ." John said gently. "I mean, it'd be natural as could be if you were mad about everybody pokin' their noses around. And we figgered maybe . . ." His voice faded away.

"You're my friends," Edward said sadly, "but you don't believe me when I tell you the plain truth. That's a sorry pickle, ain't it?"

"How come you went out today with your gun, then?" Clara challenged. "You told us you'd never ever use that gun again as long as you lived."

"Sometimes a man's gotta change his mind." Edward shook his head. "And I didn't count on Bird's-Eye Taylor."

"What do you mean, Edward?" Christy asked.

"Let's get that ankle o' yours wrapped up," Edward said.

"And on your way down the mountain, I'll show you just what I mean."

❧ Fifteen ❧

We're almost there now," Edward said.

They were halfway down the mountain. It had been slow going for Christy. But hobbling along with John and Edward for support, she felt certain she could make it all the way down.

After a few more minutes, Edward led them through thick underbrush to a spot by a tiny stream. "There," he said, pointing. "That's why I was packin' my ol' Colt forty-five."

"A still?" Christy cried.

"And there's plenty of moonshine to go with it," Edward added. "It's hidden under those bushes, mostly."

"How long has this been here?"

"Couldn't have been here long, I reckon. I know this mountain like the back o' my hand." Edward stroked his long beard. "First time I seen Bird's-Eye was a few days ago. Sneakin' 'round here like a low-bellied snake, he was."

"How can you know for certain it was Bird's-Eye?" Christy asked.

"Edward knows just about everybody," Clara explained. "On account o' we described 'em all."

Edward chuckled. "I'll bet I've heard more tales about the folks in Cutter Gap than they've heard about me."

"So you were out with your gun today lookin' for Bird's-Eye?" Fairlight asked.

"He comes just around nightfall mostly, near as I can tell. I was goin' to stake out a hidin' place, maybe shoot a couple rounds into the air to scare him off. I only want just to scare him," Edward said, his face suddenly grave. "You know how I feel about usin' my gun anymore."

"Edward was an Indian fighter, way back in the eighteen-seventies, Miz Christy," Clara said. "That's how he lost his ear and got all scarred up. He fought with—"

"That's enough, Clara," Edward interrupted sternly.

Clara bit her lip. "Sorry, Edward. I sorta forgot you don't like talkin' about it."

Christy considered pressing him for more information, but she could tell from Edward's icy tone that now was not the time.

"Well, I guess when I get home, I'll have to tell David and the others about this still," she said. "Then they can confront Bird's-Eye. There's no point in trying to scare Bird's-Eye off with some gunshots into the air, Edward. It would just start up a little war on this mountain. Bird's-Eye Taylor's spent his whole life feuding."

"Maybe you're right. Maybe the mission folks can fix things better than I can. But you won't go tellin' 'em about me," Edward said softly. It was more of a question than a demand.

"I suppose not, Edward. Not if you don't want me to. But I don't see—"

"Look, I just want my mountain back," Edward said. "I just want my peace. I've been here so many years . . ."

"How long *have* you been here?"

"So long, to tell you truthful, I can't remember."

"That must be how the rumors started so many years ago," Christy said. "People would catch a glimpse of you now and then, and one thing led to another. . . . Of course, that doesn't explain all the recent incidents."

"That still tells you all you need to know about the culprit."

"Bird's-Eye? Yes, that thought crossed my mind, too," Christy said. "But then I remembered that Bird's-Eye's son—"

"Lundy," Edward interrupted. "He's the

meanest bully in Tennessee." He winked at Clara and John. "Am I right?"

"You're right as rain," Clara said. "See, Miz Christy? He knows everybody."

Christy smiled. "Yes, he certainly does. Anyway, Lundy was helping the men work on telephone poles when somebody threw a hornet's nest at them. If Bird's-Eye were the one doing the pranks, I'm sure Lundy would have been in on it. So why would he have put himself in harm's way like that?"

"He was one o' the first to run, Miz Christy," Clara pointed out. "Maybe he was just tryin' to make him and his pa look innocent."

"I don't know," John said. "That's awfully smart for ol' Lundy."

"Wait a minute," Christy said. "How come you knew Lundy was the first to run away?"

"We was watchin'," Clara admitted. "Pokin' around, tryin' to figger out who was causin' all the Boggin trouble."

John met Edward's gaze. "Truth is, Edward, we was afeared it was you. But we was always a-hopin' we was wrong."

Edward nodded. "I s'pose that's all I could ask for from a friend. And then some." He gave a little smile. "I just want you to know I don't mind the telephone wires comin' over the mountain. Wires don't scare me. People do. I don't want no Bird's-Eye Taylors and their like disturbin' my peace. But the preacher and his telephone-makin' . . . well, that don't matter to me, I s'pose. That'll come and go, soon enough."

As they neared the main path at the foot of the mountain, Edward hung back. "Can you all make it the rest o' the way?" he asked. "This is as far as I should go."

"We'll be fine," Christy said.

"You're welcome to come a-visitin' again. As long as you don't bring nobody with you but John and Clara and their ma."

"I just might take you up on that offer. And thank you, Edward, for all your help."

"I didn't mind so much," Edward said. "I ain't helped nobody but the birds in so long . . . it was kinda nice."

Christy and the others watched him weave back through the trees. Funny, Christy mused, the way Edward thought of Boggin Mountain as his own. Just the way she felt the soothing sight of it was somehow "hers." Peculiar as he was, he clearly loved this quiet place.

"I wonder if he's right about Bird's-Eye," Christy said.

"I figger Edward's a good man, Christy," Fairlight said thoughtfully. "He's a gentle soul. I don't think he'd ever try to scare anyone."

"No, that's the kind of behavior you'd expect to see from Bird's-Eye Taylor," Christy agreed.

"And Lundy," Clara added.

"You know," Christy said, "if it really has been Bird's-Eye behind these incidents, what he needs is a dose of his own medicine."

"I'd give anything to see him and ol' Lundy scared silly!" Clara exclaimed.

Suddenly, Christy had a very clever, very interesting, very amusing thought.

"John," she said, "run on back and get Edward. Tell him I have an idea that just might interest him."

❧ Sixteen ❧

Look at all of you!" Miss Ida scolded. "You look like something the cat dragged in!"

Christy, Fairlight, Clara, and John were gathered in the mission house parlor. Miss Ida had made them hot tea, and David was putting the finishing touches on a fire in the hearth. Miss Alice had found cozy quilts for each of the rain-drenched mountain climbers.

"I'm so sorry about your coat, Miss Ida," Christy said. "I feel just terrible—"

"Nonsense. A coat's a coat, a person's a person. The important thing is that you're all right," Miss Ida said, in a rare moment of sentiment. "Still," she added brusquely, returning to her old self, "I can't imagine why you chose today to go for a walk in the mountains!"

"It just felt like something I had to do," Christy explained.

She hadn't told anyone that the mountain she'd been climbing was Boggin Mountain, and fortunately, nobody had asked. Like Fairlight, she felt obligated to protect Edward's privacy. Still, in her heart, it made her sad to think of him all alone in that little, silent hut.

"Well, we should be heading on home," Fairlight said, getting to her feet. "Jeb's goin' to be wonderin' what's happened to us. You take care of that ankle now, Christy."

"I will. Don't forget we're getting together tomorrow evening for another walk in the woods."

"Christy!" Miss Alice exclaimed. "Don't you think you should stay off that foot for a few days?"

"I'll be fine, Miss Alice." Christy winked at Fairlight and the children. "Tomorrow, then?"

"Tomorrow," Fairlight said, waving. "We'll be there." John and Clara exchanged knowing looks and grinned from ear to ear as they followed their mother out the door.

"They're in a mighty fine mood," David said as he closed the door behind them. He sighed. "At least *some*body is."

"David," Miss Alice said kindly. "Please stop thinking about that telephone. Perhaps down the road in a few months, when things have calmed down, you can try again."

"Or even sooner," Christy said with a secret smile. "Who knows?"

"I feel like a real, live spy!" Clara whispered the next evening.

"Hush!" John chided. "Real, live spies know how to keep their mouths shut."

Christy, Fairlight, Edward, and the two oldest Spencer children were crouched behind bushes, near the little stream where Bird's-Eye had put his still. It was twilight, and the woods were shrouded in shadows.

"You did some scoutin' when you were in the Seventh Cavalry, Edward," Clara said. "I could be a spy, couldn't I?"

"You'd make a fine spy, Clara," Edward said, his eyes glued on the still.

Christy thought back to her history lessons for a moment. The Seventh Cavalry? Why did that ring a bell?

She started to ask, but just then, the sound of rustling nearby silenced her.

Crouching low, they all waited, holding their breath.

"False alarm," Edward announced after a moment. He pointed toward a blur of movement in the trees. "It's just a curious doe."

"Maybe we should go over our plan again," Fairlight said. "Does everybody know what they need to be doin'?"

"We done went over it a hundred times already, Ma," Clara complained.

Fairlight laughed. "All right. I'm sorry. Guess I'm not used to bein' so sneaky." She nudged Christy. "How's that ankle o' yours holdin' up?"

"The swelling's down. It's practically back to normal," Christy replied. "Edward, do you think it's about time to take your place?"

He nodded. "I got my kerosene lamp and my sheet."

"You be careful not to catch yourself on fire," Christy warned. "John, have you got your paper cone?"

"Just like the one you made for the telephones, Miz Christy. Only bigger."

"And Fairlight and Clara and I have plenty of Miss Ida's kitchen utensils. All right, then. I think we're all set. You sure you can make it up into the tree all right, Edward?"

"John'll give me a hand. 'Sides, I may be old, but I'm spry as they come." Edward stood. "Well, here we go. You really think this'll work?"

"Just remember," Christy said. "Tonight, you're not Edward Hinton. You're the Boggin."

Edward laughed. "I might as well be him. Everybody figgers I am, anyways!"

Edward climbed into position. John stationed himself nearby, behind a tree. Christy, Fairlight, and the children made certain they were well-hidden by bushes.

The sky was darkening fast. Already a few stray stars blinked through the trees. The leaves whispered softly.

Before long, the sound of footsteps and loud voices floated on the air.

"Here they come," John whispered. "Keep low—" he glared at Clara, "and no more talkin'!"

"What I needs," came a gravelly voice Christy recognized as Bird's-Eye's, "is to find myself a hundred o' them hornets' nests. Better 'n cannonballs, they is!"

The next voice was Lundy's. "Funniest thing I ever did see, all them folks a-runnin' like scared rabbits!"

Bird's-Eye and Lundy reached the still. "Think I'll have a swig or two o' brew before we get to work," Bird's-Eye said. He jerked an elbow at Lundy. "What're you lookin' for, boy? Ain't nobody comes to this mountain but us."

"Us and . . . and the Boggin," Lundy said nervously.

Bird's-Eye spat on the ground. "Fool! You and me *is* the Boggin!"

"Still and all, Pa, there's folks who say they've seen him, lurkin' around these parts."

Bird's-Eye gave a sharp laugh. "My uncle once swore he saw a three-headed mule. You think I believed him?"

Suddenly, an eerie light appeared, high up

in the branches of an oak tree. Above the white glow, a face scowled.

"Believe this, Bird's-Eye Taylor!" came a deep voice.

"There is only one Boggin! And here I am!"

✎ Seventeen ✎

P a?" Lundy whispered, grabbing Bird's-Eye's arm. "That there is the Boggin, for sure and certain! And he's every bit as ugly as they say!"

Christy and Fairlight smiled at each other. Edward had draped the white sheet around his neck. With the kerosene lamp glowing beneath the sheet, his body seemed to glow. The effect was terrifying.

"Let go o' my arm, boy! I'll shoot him right outa that tree!"

Christy looked at Fairlight in terror. She'd been so sure of her plan to scare Bird's-Eye. It hadn't occurred to her that he might actually try to shoot Edward.

"Shoot me if you will," John called through his paper cone. "But every shot you take, I'll spin that bullet clear around to take aim right at you!"

"Good job, John," Christy whispered.

Bird's-Eye hesitated. In the dim light, the fear on his face was obvious. He took a step back.

"He's talkin'," he said in a hoarse voice to Lundy, "but his lips ain't movin' none. How in tarnation can he do that?"

"He's the *Boggin*, Pa," Lundy squeaked. "He can do anything he wants!"

"Destroy your still now!" John boomed from his hiding place behind the tree. "And pour out your moonshine!"

"I . . . I can't do that," Bird's-Eye pleaded. "It's fine moonshine, the finest in Tennessee, uh . . . Mr. Boggin, sir. How about I just split it with you, nice and fair?"

"Destroy it now! Or I'll give you a taste o' my Boggin powers!"

Bird's-Eye shook his head. "How do you do that, if'n you don't mind my askin'? Talk without openin' your mouth, I mean?"

"Pour out the moonshine! Now!"

Christy nudged Fairlight and Clara. They began pounding pots and pans together, clanging and clattering like crazy. At the same time, they howled like wolves baying at the moon. It was such a horrible racket, Christy wished she'd brought ear plugs. But the effect was just what she'd hoped.

"All right! I—I'll do it!" Bird's-Eye cried in terror. Lundy clamped his hands to his ears. "J—just stop all that carryin'-on!"

Christy gave a nod and the commotion ceased instantly.

After that, the only noise was a steady glug-glug-glug, as Bird's-Eye and Lundy poured out bottle after bottle of their precious moonshine. Christy watched in delight as they dismantled the still, tossing pieces into the dark woods.

"There," Bird's-Eye said at last. "I hope you're satisfied, Mr. Boggin."

"I am satisfied," John said, "but there is one thing more."

"Confound it all," Bird's-Eye muttered. "You sure do know how to ruin a fella's evening."

"You must go to the people of Cutter Gap. You must tell them if they help with the telephone they will not be harmed. And you must confess that you're the one who's been scarin' 'em so."

"Aw, come on, Mr. Boggin. Ain't I done enough already?"

"Pa," Lundy pleaded. "Don't make him any madder 'n he already is!"

Bird's-Eye scowled. "All right, then. If'n you say so." With a sigh, he turned to go. "I never did like this mountain, anyways."

They were almost out of sight when John added, "By the way, Lundy—you really oughta stop pickin' on the little children at school."

"Nosy ol' Boggin," Lundy muttered. "Fella can't have a lick o' fun with him around."

❧ Eighteen ❧

The next week, when her ankle had fully healed, Christy returned to Boggin Mountain.

She found Edward near his hut, carving another birdhouse. Little curlicues of wood carpeted the ground, and the fresh smell of cut wood filled the air. He seemed surprised, and perhaps even a little pleased, to see her.

"I hope you don't mind my coming back, Edward," she said, taking a seat on a log.

"'Course not. You're welcome any time, like I said."

"That's a fine birdhouse."

Edward held it out at arm's length. "My birdhouses now are not as fine as they used to be. I'm gettin' on, I s'pose. My hands get tired and my eyes do, too."

"You know, there's a store back home in Asheville, where I come from. They sell handmade things, quilts and pottery and such. I'll bet you anything they'd be willing to sell your birdhouses, too."

Edward looked at her doubtfully, as if he thought she were making fun of him. "Naw."

"Seriously. I could send one to my mother, if you'd like. She could show it to the shop owner."

Edward shrugged. "Ain't got enough for sellin'."

"Suppose . . . suppose you taught some of the local people how to carve them? They could help you—"

"I done told you. I don't want nothin' to do with nobody."

"I'm sorry," Christy said. "I didn't mean to push you. Especially since the real reason I came was to say thanks."

Edward blew wood shavings off the birdhouse. They fluttered to his feet like bits of snow. "Thank me for what?"

"For helping us get Bird's-Eye to destroy his still and pour out his moonshine."

"He'll build another 'un, mark my words."

"Perhaps. But not on your mountain, at least. And he admitted he was behind the pranks, like we asked. You'd be amazed how fast word spread about that. He explained everything. How he'd put chicken blood on one of his own tattered shirts and hung it in the tree. How he'd made the big tracks using a piece of wood he'd carved and an old pitchfork. It's like I told the children—there's a logical explanation for everything." Christy laughed. "He told everyone he'd seen you, too, but I'm not sure anyone believed him. It was sort of like that old story about the boy who cried wolf one too many times."

Edward set the birdhouse aside. "Telephone line's a-comin', then?"

"Yes. They're making real progress on the poles already."

"I'd best be goin' into hidin' for a while, till they're done and gone."

Gently, Christy reached for the little birdhouse. It was only half-done, but she could already see the outlines forming. "It's the church!" she said.

"I reckon."

"You've seen it?"

"Once. 'Round midnight, right after the preacher was finishin' it up. Fine job he did."

"He'd be pleased to hear that. David doesn't fashion himself much of a carpenter. I think he'd rather stick to being a minister." She smiled. "You'd like him."

"Maybe."

"I wish you'd come visit us at the mission house sometime. Everyone would love to meet you."

Edward stared up at the pale blue sky. "Ain't likely."

With a sigh, Christy set the birdhouse

down. "I know this is none of my business, Edward. But the other night while we were waiting for Bird's-Eye, Clara mentioned the Seventh Cavalry. At the time, I couldn't remember its significance. But later, when I got home, I took out my history book, and all of a sudden it came back to me." She paused, almost afraid to say the words. "The Seventh Cavalry fought the Battle of Little Big Horn—Custer's Last Stand."

Edward gave a slight nod. He was looking at Christy, but his milky eyes were somewhere far, far away. "I ran from that bloody place in the Dakota Territory. And I never looked back. I been here on my mountain ever since."

"So many died that day," Christy said softly.

"I was ridin' with Major Reno. There was one hundred and twelve of us troops, green as new grass. We attacked the Sioux at one end of the Indian camp, and a fool thing it was, too. We was way outnumbered. The fightin' was . . ." he winced at the awful memory, "somethin' terrible. Lookin' back, I think those Sioux just wanted to be left alone on the land they loved, same as me. But I didn't know that then."

"It must have been horrible."

"Ain't no words to describe it. I saw men, troops and Indians alike, fight brave as you can imagine. In the end, Major Reno pulled us back, what was left of us. Some called him a coward." He sighed. "S'pose that's what they'd call me, too. Soon as I got the chance, I run off. I was just a boy, mind you. Bloody and tired and scared o' dyin'. Later, I heard about Custer and his men. Two hundred sixty-four troops, all dead. All those lives, wasted."

A lone tear fell down Edward's cheek. Christy reached out and touched his hand. "Edward," she said gently, "that was a long time ago. Haven't you suffered enough?"

"Maybe so. But it's been too long. I don't know how to be around people anymore."

"Sure you do."

"Even old men can be afraid, you know." He managed a half-smile. "Even the Boggin."

"I know a little about fear myself," Christy admitted. "Truth is, that day you found me pinned under the tree, I'd come up here to prove something to myself."

"Prove something?"

"I was afraid of *you*, Edward . . . or at least of the thing everyone called the Boggin. And it made me mad, and sad, too, because if I was afraid of you, that meant I had to be afraid of this beautiful mountain, too." She paused. "And I loved this place too much to let that happen."

Edward nodded. "I'm glad you were brave

enough to come. But I'm not like that. I'm somebody who learned how to run away a long, long time ago. And now it's too late."

"You ran away from the worst side of human nature, Edward. And believe me, it's never too late to change."

"Maybe so. Maybe not. You know what they say about teaching old dogs new tricks."

"I taught my poodle Pansy to roll over when she was twelve years old and fat as one of the hogs living under the schoolhouse."

Edward laughed. "You're comparin' me to a fat ol' poodle dog?"

"Hardly." Christy stood. "Edward, do you suppose you still have family living?"

"I had a younger sister in Raleigh. Could be she's still around. Mary Davis was her name, after she got hitched."

"Wouldn't you like to get in touch with her?"

Edward shook his head. "I'm afraid I just plain wouldn't know where to begin, if I did."

"I understand. Well, I should be going. But will you at least think about visiting the mission someday?"

"I'll think about it. That's all I'm promisin'."

"It wouldn't be like visiting strangers. After all, you already know about everyone in Cutter Gap. Don't you think they'd like to know about you?"

"I ain't so sure." Edward went over to the nearest pine tree. He pulled down a little birdhouse. "Here. This ain't got no residents yet. Send it on to your ma to show to the shopkeeper, if'n you want. I ain't promisin' anything, mind you. I'm old and stuck in my ways."

Christy grinned. "Funny—that's just what everyone said about Pansy."

❧ Nineteen ❧

Nine weeks later . . .

"I can hardly stand the waitin' another minute!" Clara cried.

"Settle down, Clara," Ruby Mae teased. "This ain't the first call we've got."

"Practically, though," Clara said. "'Sides, it's the first one that's come from out o' state. And it's the first one we've had such a big jollification over."

She gazed around the mission house happily. It seemed like all of Cutter Gap was here for the big occasion. The parlor was decorated with vases of wildflowers. Pies and cookies were waiting to be eaten. And all over the walls were pictures the children had drawn—pictures of the way they imagined the Boggin would look when they finally got to meet him today.

She adjusted the bow in her hair nervously. Miz Christy had given it to her in honor of the special day.

"Quit playin' with that bow or it'll fall right apart," John teased.

Clara punched him in the arm. "John, you think he'll really come? Miz Christy said he was powerful scared."

"He's come to the mission house twice now," John pointed out.

"'Course, there was only a few people to visit with then. Everybody in Cutter Gap is here today."

Suddenly, a hush fell over the room. Every head turned toward the door.

Edward stood in the doorway. He bit his lip, staring at the huge assembled group.

Clara could see the panic in his eyes. She rushed over and took his hand. "Everybody," she announced, nice and firm and proud as could be, "this is my friend, Edward Hinton." She pulled him inside. "You're late, Edward. I was afeared you weren't a-goin' to come, and Miz Christy and the preacher fixed up the finest surprise you ever did—"

Then it happened, right on schedule. The brand-new, fine-as-could-be telephone began to ring.

A hush fell over the crowd.

It rang again, a jangly, silvery noise like tiny bells coming alive.

"Confound it all, if that ain't the most beautiful sound I ever did hear!" someone cried.

"Ain't somebody goin' to answer it?" Granny O'Teale demanded.

"Edward, why don't you do the honors?" said Christy. She gave a sly little wink at Clara.

"I don't think . . . I don't know if I'm ready for . . ."

"Come, come, there's nothing to it." David led Edward toward the phone.

"Just pick up that earpiece and say 'hello,'" Clara explained. "Miz Christy done taught us all how."

Edward hesitated. Again the phone jangled.

"Hurry up!" someone hissed. "Or they'll give up on you!"

With a trembling hand, Edward lifted the earpiece and put it to his ear.

"Talk into that cone-shaped thing," Clara whispered.

Edward cleared his throat. "H—hello?"

He listened. His eyes went wide.

More long moments passed. Clara waited, breath held.

"Mary?" Edward whispered. "Mary, is that really you?"

Clara reached for Miz Christy's hand and squeezed it tightly. They both smiled.

"Finally, Miz Christy," Clara whispered, "he ain't the Boggin no more."

About the Author

Catherine Marshall

With *Christy*, Catherine Marshall LeSourd (1914–1983) created one of the world's most widely read and best-loved classics. Published in 1967, the book spent 39 weeks on the New York Times bestseller list. With an estimated 30 million Americans having read it, *Christy* is now approaching its 90th printing and has sold more than eight million copies. Although a novel, *Christy* is in fact a thinly-veiled biography of Catherine's mother, Leonora Wood.

Catherine Marshall LeSourd also authored *A Man Called Peter*, which has sold more than four million copies. It is an American bestseller, portraying the love between a dynamic man and his God, and the tender, romantic love between a man and the girl he married.

Another of Catherine's books is *Julie,* a powerful, sweeping novel of love and adventure, courage and commitment, tragedy and triumph, in a Pennsylvania town during the Great Depression. Catherine also authored many other devotional books of encouragement.

THE CHRISTY® FICTION SERIES

You'll want to read them all!

Based upon Catherine Marshall's international bestseller Christy®, this new series contains expanded adventures filled with romance, intrigue, and excitement.

#1—The Bridge to Cutter Gap

Nineteen-year-old Christy leaves her family to teach at a mission school in the Great Smoky Mountains. On the other side of an icy bridge lie excitement, adventure, and maybe even the man of her dreams . . . but can she survive a life-and-death struggle when she falls into the rushing waters below? (ISBN 0-8499-3686-1)

#2—Silent Superstitions

Christy's students are suddenly afraid to come to school. Is what Granny O' Teale says true? Is their teacher cursed? Will the children's fears and the adults' superstitions force Christy to abandon her dreams and return to North Carolina? (ISBN 0-8499-3687-X)

#3—The Angry Intruder

Someone wants Christy to leave Cutter Gap, and they'll stop at nothing. Mysterious pranks soon turn dangerous. Could a student be the culprit? When Christy confronts the late-night intruder, will it be a face she knows? (ISBN 0-8499-3688-8)

#4—Midnight Rescue

The mission's black stallion, Prince, has vanished, and so has Christy's student Ruby Mae. Christy must brave the guns of angry moonshiners to bring them home. Will her faith in God see her through her darkest night? (ISBN 0-8499-3689-6)

#5—The Proposal
Christy should be thrilled when David Grantland, the handsome minister, proposes marriage, but her feelings of excitement are mixed with confusion and uncertainty. Several untimely interruptions delay her answer to David's proposal. Then a terrible riding accident and blindness threaten all of Christy's dreams for the future.
(ISBN 0-8499-3918-6)

#6—Christy's Choice
When Christy is offered a chance to teach in her hometown, she faces a difficult decision. Will her train ride back to Cutter Gap be a journey home or a last farewell? In a moment of terror and danger, Christy must decide where her future lies.
(ISBN 0-8499-3919-4)

#7—The Princess Club
When Ruby Mae, Bessie, and Clara discover gold at Cutter Gap, they form an exclusive organization, "The Princess Club." Christy watches in dismay as her classroom—and her community—are torn apart by greed, envy, and an understanding of what true wealth really means.
(ISBN 0-8499-3958-5)

#8—Family Secrets
Bob Allen and many of the residents of Cutter Gap are upset when a black family, the Washingtons, moves in near the Allens' property. When a series of threatening incidents befall the

Washingtons, Christy steps in to help. But it's a clue in the Washingtons' family Bible that may hold the real key to peace and acceptance. (ISBN 0-8499-3959-3)

#9—Mountain Madness
When Christy travels alone to a nearby mountain, she vows to discover the truth behind the terrifying legend of a strange mountain creature. But what she finds at first seems worse than she ever imagined! (ISBN 0-8499-3960-7)

#10—Stage Fright
As Christy's students are preparing for a school play, she reveals her dream to act on stage herself. Little does she know that Doctor MacNeill's aunt is the artistic director of the Knoxville theater. Before long, just as Christy is about to debut on stage, several mysterious incidents threaten both her dreams and her pride! (ISBN 0-8499-3961-5)

Christy is now available on home videos through Broadman & Holman Publishers.

Stage Fright

Book Ten in the Christy® Fiction Series

Christy was so busy working on her lines backstage that she barely noticed the small figure reflected in the mirror.

"Oliver?" she asked, spinning around.

"I'm sorry to disturb you," he muttered. "I left my hat in here the other day, when I departed in such a huff." He poked around in a pile of costumes. "No matter. It's not as if anyone cares whether my head is warm. I'm sure they'd all be thrilled if I caught cold and expired."

"Oliver, don't say that. I can tell the cast is very fond of you."

"Fond! Phooey! They hate me, all of them. And of course they *love* Cora. Sure, Cora is the perfect director. All I heard while she was away was, 'Why can't you be more like Cora, Oliver?' Well, I'm not Cora! I'm Oliver! Oliver Flump!"

"Of course you are."

"She'll get her comeuppance, soon enough."

"What do you mean?" Christy asked, frowning.

"I mean this play will fall apart at the seams, and then we'll see who the true director is!

Well, I must be off. I'm not wanted here."
Christy watched him go.

"Christy!" Arabella poked her head in the door. "Cora's calling for you."

"Here I come," Christy said, but as she stood up, a horrible ripping sound met her ears.

"It's glued!" Christy cried. "Somebody put glue on my chair!"

"Goodness, this *is* unfortunate. I'm not sure I've got another spare skirt."

"Well, I can't go out on stage with my petticoat showing," Christy said frantically.

"Let me see what I can rustle up. You stay put."

A few minutes later, Arabella returned. She was carrying something shiny and stiff. It looked like a pair of men's trousers, made of metal.

"What on earth is that?" Christy asked.

"Armor. From our last play, *Joan of Arc*. I think it'll fit you nicely."

Christy crossed her arms over her chest.

"This is ridiculous. There must be something else I can—"

"Christy!" Marylou appeared at the door. "You'd better hurry! Everybody's waitin'!"

"When there's a crisis in the theater, we all do our part," Arabella told Christy. "You must try to be cooperative."

"Oh, all right. I'll wear it."

Moments later, Christy clunked her way onto the stage. Her armor-covered legs were so stiff she could barely move. She was greeted with gales of laughter.

"Interesting fashion choice," said Aunt Cora, grinning. "But I don't think it's quite Juliet's style."

"My dress ripped," Christy said sullenly. She didn't think there was any point in explaining how it had ripped. If a practical joker *had* deliberately put glue on her chair, she didn't want to give that person the satisfaction of seeing her upset.

"Well, let's proceed. We've got a lot to cover today. Let's start with the scene in Capulet's orchard."

Aunt Cora pointed to a group of wooden trees in the center of the stage. They were five tall pieces of wood, cut and painted to resemble apple trees. A wooden stand at the base kept each tree erect.

"Juliet—I mean, Christy—you'll enter first from stage left, followed by the nurse."

Christy did as she was told. *Clank. Clank. Clank.* Every step made a horrible noise, but Christy was determined to struggle on. Behind her, she could hear the whispers and gigles of her fellow cast members.

"Fine. Stop there," Aunt Cora directed.

"Now, let's hear your lines. Try to direct your voice even farther than yesterday. This is an awfully big theater, so you need to project."

Christy cleared her throat. "Gallop apace, you fiery-footed steeds—" she began.

"Even louder, dear," Aunt Cora called.

"Gallop apace, you fiery-footed—"

"Look out!" someone yelled.

Suddenly, as if in slow motion, the apple tree behind Christy began to fall. Christy lurched sideways, out of its path. The movement was too sudden for her metal-clad legs.

There was no way to regain her balance. With a horrible thud, Christy landed on her backside, as the apple tree toppled to the floor, only inches away.

"Christy!" Are you all right?" Gilroy ran to her side.

"I'm fine," Christy admitted with a shaky laugh.

"I want somebody to explain to me what just happened," Aunt Cora said sternly.

One of the stagehands examined the tree. "There's a rope attached to the bottom of this prop tree. Somebody must have yanked on it. I'm awful sorry, Christy."

"Don't worry about it," Christy said, "I'm fine. However, it may take the entire cast to help me stand up in this armor."

"I feel terrible about this," Aunt Cora said. "Here you are, doing your best to help us out, and somebody's pulling these silly pranks."

"I'll say one thing. I'm starting to get the feeling somebody doesn't want me to star in this play," Christy said with a grim smile.